Major League Murder

Gun sat up, trying to unmuck his brain.

"It's a hell of a surprise, isn't it?" said Coach, waving his piece of steel, which Gun now saw was a cattle prod. "Volts, amps, I don't know. Don't pay no attention. What I know is, ain't a steer I ever worked with didn't live in mortal dread of this thing." With a fleetness that belied his size, the fat man thrust the prod at Gun. Gun parried with a forearm, and the roll of electricity sucked his breath from him, peeled back his nerves like a sleeve. He felt the swamp crust shake when his head hit it, and lying there, he smelled burned skin.

"Ought to have stayed outa the swamp, anyhow," Coach said . . .

"L. L. Enger is a terrific writer. . . . *SWING* is a sure hit."

—R.D. Zimmerman, author of
Deadfall in Berlin

"In *SWING*, the plot twists as unpredictably as a hangman's rope. *SWING* has muscle (and heart, too)."

—Mary Cannon Trone,
Alfred Hitchcock's Mystery Magazine

Books by L. L. Enger

Comeback
Swing

Published by POCKET BOOKS

SWING

A GUN PEDERSEN MYSTERY

L.L. ENGER

POCKET BOOKS

New York   London   Toronto   Sydney   Tokyo   Singapore

This book is a work of fiction. Names, characters, places and incidents are either the product of the author's imagination or are used fictitiously. Any resemblance to actual events or locales or persons, living or dead, is entirely coincidental.

An *Original* Publication of POCKET BOOKS

POCKET BOOKS, a division of Simon & Schuster Inc.
1230 Avenue of the Americas, New York, NY 10020

Copyright © 1991 by Leif and Lin Enger

ISBN: 0-671-70919-4

First Pocket Books printing August 1991

10 9 8 7 6 5 4 3 2 1

POCKET and colophon are registered trademarks of
Simon & Schuster Inc.

Printed in the U.S.A.

For Ty and Hope

1

The northern pike came in hard from the east and struck the red-and-white decoy without caution or apparent effort. The decoy disappeared under ice, traveled with the pike to the limit of its monofilament line, and sprang back. Its tin tail fin was crumpled. Flakes of red paint drifted down to settle on the sandy lake floor. In eight feet of green glass the decoy hung still, listing to the right, in shock. The pike was gone.

"Twenty pounds and growing," said Gun Pedersen. He shook his head and leaned the black four-pointed fishing spear against the wall of the shack. The afternoon was getting old; the two-foot square of open water wasn't letting much light into the windowless spear house anymore. Gun stood and stretched, glad again he'd built the house himself instead of buying it from someone who wasn't six and a half feet high. He took the red Prince Albert can from its place on the wall and patted his pocket. No papers. There was coffee, though, bitter from an afternoon on the gas stove. He poured some into a white glass mug with green letters that said MILO'S YOUR HAPPY CHAIN SAW MAN and stepped out to watch the sun go under.

He didn't get to see it. First thing, a long black snow cloud ranged in from the north and covered the spot of horizon where the sun was about to land, and then Gun heard a thin scraping sound coming from the shack.

The fish was back. The big pike. Nuzzling the red-and-white decoy like he was sorry he'd hurt it so bad the first time, and the monofilament was moving against the edge of the shack's cutout floor. Gun reached for the spear, slowly, *don't scare him,* gripped it, went to one knee for leverage. *Twenty pounds. Bigger.* He lowered the spear until the barbed iron tips were an inch below the surface. For half a minute the fish moved around, flirting, in and out of Gun's vision. Forty seconds. *Light's getting bad, stay still, there now, stay right there*—and then a tiny but meaningful tremor touched the ice, and the water rose slightly in the hole, and the big pike fled. At the same time Gun felt the hum of an engine and wheels. There were more ice tremors. The engine moved in nearer, settled up next to the shack and died. He heard the loose clank of car metal and knew it would be Jack LaSalle in his old Scout. He blew out the breath he'd held for the fish, understanding there'd be no such chance again. He forced the thought to fade, filled the Happy Chain Saw mug for Jack and set it on the stove.

See any whales?" Jack said. He'd entered the shack without knocking and picked up the coffee without looking.

"Missed one, just before you got here," Gun said mildly. "Big one." He handed Jack the sorrowful decoy.

Jack sat on a canvas camp stool by the stove and squinted in the quickly dying light. He took off leather mittens and felt the ruined tail fin with his fingers. He sniffed it briefly, as if winding pike. He said, "Moby." Then the sun went for good and the only light in the

2

house was a residual glimmer from the spearing hole that turned LaSalle into a squat dark roundness in the corner. He was nearly as tall sitting as he was standing; he'd pushed back the hood of his parka, and its fringe of gray wolf fur glistened on his shoulders. He carried with him primal smells, oak fire and red meat and beer. He swallowed coffee. "Reason I came, Gun, Moses Gates is trying to get ahold of you."

It should have been good news. The edge in Jack's voice said it wasn't.

"Moses? I haven't seen him since the Twins traded him to California. After fifteen good years," Gun said.

"Well, he's in Palm Beach now. Evidently tried calling your house, and when you weren't there he called the post office in Stony. Only number he could think of, I suppose. So then that kid Freddy leaves the mail desk, hangs up a sign says postal emergency or something and comes whaling out to my place. I got customers, mind you, I got five big burgers going, and Freddy comes in all important, 'I gotta find Mr. Pedersen.' 'Not here,' I say, 'Probably out on the ice.' " A grin came into Jack's voice. "Poor Freddy. His chance to be the courier for news of great portent, and you're out of reach."

"I'm guessing you'll get around to Moses," Gun said.

Jack handed across a slip of paper. "I don't think it was the sort of message Moses really wanted to leave with the mail boy."

Gun lit a match on the stove top and read. "Another one is dead, and I could use a hand." Then a phone number. Gun rested his head against the wall of the shack.

Last he'd heard of Gates, the old catcher was back in baseball. Sort of. He was managing one of those old-timer teams down in Florida, where they had a special league for ballplayers who'd gone broke, or got cut, or just couldn't let the game go. He didn't know

3

which group Gates belonged to. Hadn't talked with him, not in years. He said, "You remember that Gates business, Jack?"

"Not very well. Late seventies, wasn't it? There was that outfielder, Ferdie something, got strung up in Tinker Field during spring training."

"Ferdie Millevich," Gun said. "Played some nice left field for the Twins and was starting to swing nice, too. Then after practice one day the janitor was turning off the power and found him hanging from the press box. Just dangling there, out over the lower-deck seats. Used an electrical cord."

"I remember they thought Gates did it."

Gun cast back in his mind and started reeling in the details. They came too easily. "It made good headlines. Gates and Millevich'd had some tough words, and the wrong people heard them. Moses didn't have an alibi handy, either, which didn't help." Gun shut his eyes in the dark. "You want to go home, get out of everybody's sight once in a while, you know? Moses had the bad luck to do that at the wrong time. Nobody could vouch for him, so all the reporters naturally figured he was out killing someone instead. They were on him, it was like lizards on a cool rock."

"Wasn't it suicide, though?"

"Coroner said so, and the grand jury believed him. What happens, though, Moses goes through an investigation that the papers run day-by-day, like Dagwood. He's got half a dozen fans left defending him and everybody else in the country calling him Hangman Gates. And then the coroner steps in and says suicide, Moses didn't do it, so all the lizards jump off the rock and scatter, only you know what?"

Jack waited.

"The damn lizards have crapped all over the rock. So you wait. You wait and hope that time and weather will get rid of the stains. But they hang on." Gun stopped. Talking of his friend made him feel as though he'd backed up into his own life. "All you can do," he finished uncomfortably, "is sit absolutely still, for a long time, and hope the lizards won't notice you anymore."

In the darkness Jack lifted the empty mug and tilted it over the stove. One drop fell to the hot metal, *ssst.* "Who's dead?"

Gun stood, leaned down, cranked the gas handle hard to the left. The stove ticked, cooling. "I don't know, but it sounds like Moses is getting noticed again." He swung on his heavy wool coat and Jack followed him into the bright clear night. The winter bite entered his lungs. It would go fifteen, twenty below.

"You're going south, I guess," Jack said.

The snow cloud had disappeared from the west, leaving a solid plain of cold white stars on black heaven.

"I expect I am," Gun said.

2

He walked the mile home from the spear house because he didn't feel like bouncing over the ice in Jack's Scout and because he wanted to breathe in enough clean January to hold him for a while. The message was cryptic but clear; someone else Gates knew had died in strange circumstances, and Gates was scared the whole damned nightmare was coming back to get him.

Gun had spent his first pro year with Gates, at the

Tigers' farm team in Peoria, a year of untended scrapes and short sleeps on the bus. They'd played the same game of baseball then, ground it into their hands like dirt. Even after Gates was sent to the Twins they'd grinned and razzed each other across the diamond whenever their two teams played each other. In the spring of '77, when the mud slide started, Gun had flown to Orlando during the grand jury investigation and stolen Gates off to the coast to chase marlin for a day. They caught a few big slow turtles and drank like sea captains, and driving back, thumbed their noses at a green delivery van bearing thousands of copies of the *Orlando Evening Mail*.

Three years later Moses showed up in Detroit for the funeral of Gun's wife, Amanda; stood silently in the back of the church and didn't tell Gun not to blame himself. There were plenty of nice folks doing that already and it didn't change what Gun knew: that if he'd looked harder at his own family instead of someone else, Amanda never would have stepped on that plane and would be alive today. When he quit baseball the following week and went looking for quiet in northern Minnesota, dozens of ballplayers telegrammed him to stop wasting himself and get back to the game. Moses's telegram took six months to come, and it contained more truth than any of them. FIND THE GOOD FISHING SPOTS.

Gun reached shore and walked reluctantly up the slope to his stripped-log house. Inside he started a fire, took off his coat, found a cold steak in the fridge and laid it on bread with a slice of pale tomato. He'd eat, let the house warm up, have a smoke. And then call Moses Gates. In the kitchen the phone went off like dynamite, and he knew he wouldn't have to.

"Gun, it's Moses." The voice was deep as always, but had a nervous airiness that was new.

"I got your message."

"Sorry, man. You seemed like the guy to call, is all."

Gun let that sit a few seconds. "I'm the guy. Tell me what happened."

"A reporter, Gun. A friend of mine. Billy Apple was his name. I was supposed to meet him at his place last night. Late. I got there, knocked, no answer . . . the door was unlocked." Moses's voice was grainy, like a man's after a driving punch to the gut. His wind wasn't back yet. "He was hanging, Gun. Just like Ferdie Millevich. Only no suicide. His wrists were taped, they'd pulled a black stocking cap over his face. Billy had this big fireplace like you don't need down here. They hung him from that." He stopped a moment. "Not in*side* it, thank God."

Gun's breathing felt suddenly dry in his throat. "Any idea who?"

"No." Moses paused. "They took off Billy's shoes, man. Where they hung him, his feet were right in front of the fireplace. There was a nice big fire going when I got there. You want to know what it did, I can tell you."

"Are you in trouble, Moses?"

"Not jail trouble. This time I got an alibi, you can believe it."

"Other trouble?"

"There's a lot to it, Gun."

The kitchen clock said 7:15. Gun said, "I'll see you in the morning."

"Thanks."

He booked a 2 A.M. flight to West Palm Beach out of Minneapolis and saw Carol Long before he left. Carol edited the Stony *Journal* and accompanied Gun on occasion.

"I'm not sure I understand, Gun. Your friend Gates didn't hang this reporter. What does he have to worry about?" Carol Long was on the sofa in working clothes, black tights slender under a full-cut skirt, an

Irish sweater almost as green as her eyes. A Macintosh computer blinked on the coffee table in front of her.

"I don't know yet. At best, he's about to get a nasty visit from the Ghost of Rumors Past. At worst, well, it doesn't pay to speculate."

"You think he's in trouble?" Carol's green eyes had a wary quickness, catching Gun's when he didn't want them to.

"He almost walked into an execution, Carol. I don't know why he was meeting this Billy Apple, and I don't know who else is involved." Gun shrugged and went to the door. "That's cop business. I'm just going so he's not out there by himself."

She got up and came to him, pushing her black hair back with one hand. She had the warm smell of wool and tea and held Gun with a good toughness that surprised him.

"He's your friend, I know. But if this is the second time . . ." She looked into his face and a little fear put *Be Careful* in her eyes.

Gun gave her the easiest smile he owned. "Carol," he said, "you know what a prudent sort I am."

3

The descending DC-9 overshot West Palm Beach from the north, banked cautiously to the left and approached the airport from the ocean side, throttling back until the feeling of speed disappeared and Gun felt the plane was simply floating. It floated over a deserted freeway dimly lit by street lamps, then a line of tall hotels. "There's a big H," said the middle-aged woman next to Gun in a New York accent. "Hilton Hotel, there it is. Palm Beach is fulla green. My sister says they got hotels here, they put orchids on your pillow."

It was 5:15 A.M. A little more than a three-hour flight. "I feel like I know your sister," Gun said. And it was plain-out true.

The woman beamed. "You're going to love Palm Beach. I just know it."

The fat man at the Avis desk eyed Gun and stroked his red tie smugly, like a man with a secret. He didn't have any pickup trucks and he claimed to be fresh out of cars with leg room, but he decided to part with the secret.

"If you're not Gun Pedersen, I'm a thin man," he said.

"Sorry, that's me."

That perked Avis into a grin. "Gotta Chevy Beretta, Mr. Pedersen. Your legs'll cramp but you'll get there fast."

Gun signed for the Chevy and went to wait for the shuttle. There was a bank of pay phones and he pulled the crumpled slip from his pocket and dialed Gates's number. It rang twelve times before he hung up. He flipped up the heavy phone book and found sixteen Gateses in West Palm Beach. There was no listing for Moses but the number on Gun's scrap corresponded with that for the Gates To Home Motel. Gun scribbled the address and found it on a map between the white and yellow pages, a spot on the Intracoastal Highway just north of West Palm. Then the shuttle arrived, a great tilting glassed-in milk truck, and Gun went to face the Beretta.

It was night blue and got him to the Gates To Home Motel with not as much alacrity as the fat clerk had promised. Gun forgave him; the leg room could've been worse. It could have been as uncomfortable, say, as the motel itself looked to be. Turning in off the Intracoastal Gun saw a white, narrow, single-story building in the shape of a block U. It had a green-shingle roof that was low enough to make Gun think about ducking his head. Around the inside of the U, and not far apart, were orange doors with black painted gothic numerals, 1 through 22. There were three cars in the lot. The Beretta made four.

He stepped out and stretched. Across the highway daylight glowed on the rim, the sun maybe an hour away. He heard a low groan. A small dog was squatting in apparent pain on a patch of stiff-looking grass next to a door that said OFFICE. Over the door a tube of dead neon said GATES MOTEL—A HOME RUN VALUE. Gun thought: ballplayers.

At his fourth set of knocks a light went on somewhere behind the curtain and Gun felt steps. Another light, a merciless white one, went on right over the door and made him squint. Finally the door swung wide and Moses Gates filled it. "There ain't a way to prepare for it," Moses said. "Here I know you're coming, and I remember you've got one hell of a high profile, and it still throws me when I look out and see you standing there in the dark. You coming in?"

In the kitchen Moses stood at the stove and spooned coffee grounds. He was a middle-aged black man of medium height who'd always had the catcher's build; not narrow anywhere, just wide from legs to shoulders and straight between, like a short hardwood tree. Since Gun had seen him, though, the tree had broadened some at the trunk. Moses's belly tugged at his red T-shirt; his legs, in blue jeans, looked heavy instead of plain strong. Gun saw that his fingers were slightly unsteady on the spoon.

"I look somethin' terrible, don't I, Gun? That's another thing I can't seem to prepare for. I run this motel now for seven years, it's a business like a lot of people make a living and stay happy on. Only I can't do either. I get up every morning, my dog's outside the window trying to crap, it's the moaning wakes me up."

"You could shoot the dog, Moses."

"All these years I been keeping the old ballplayer's secret, Gun. You know the way it goes—the feeling that you quit before your time was up, that you still got your legs and your eyes. That you could still play. You've had that dream yourself."

Gun shrugged his shoulders forward, felt the shift of tired vertebrae. "A time or two."

"The Senior League's not so bad. Course some of the guys are only here because they got out of the majors before one year's salary could set you up for life. They're broke as old china, here for the money, which is lousy anyhow. The rest of 'em, hell, they've still got some good ball left in 'em. They were a shade too old or too slow for the bigs, maybe a hot kid coming up looking for their spot. So a couple hotshots decide to set up a baseball league for oldies. And we miss playing. Hell, Gun, what else did we ever do?"

"Don't apologize to me, Moses."

Moses shook his head. "But it's led to this. One day last fall I'm just another down-south motel man, poor as weak pee, and next day two guys come to me out of Orlando saying, 'We got a new team on a new league and we want you to lead it.' I'm back in baseball! And then by God people are interested in me again, I get a few calls from reporters."

"And one of them's Billy Apple."

"Said he was an old fan of mine. You live renting out cheap rooms and fixing air conditioners a few years, Gun, you start to like being reminded that you used to have things like fans." Moses glanced reluctantly at Gun. "You know the Hall vote's coming up."

"Cooperstown's just a spot on the map, Moses."

"I told myself that. Often. Hall of Fame's nothing,

11

just another page in the scrapbook. Every time the
sportswriters looked at my name on the ballot and
voted for the other guys, every damn year, that's what
I said. A spot on the map."

Gun went to a shelf of chipped white enamel and
found a clean cup. He poured coffee, hoping it would
make him glad he came.

"This Billy Apple, he's sort of a local hot dog, okay?
He's with the West Palm *By-Line,* a columnist, and
they work him loose. Mostly sports, but he does what
he wants because he does it good. Couple years ago he
writes a series on dopers in South America shipping
coke into the States. Turns out it comes in with those
soccer players, some trainer was swallowing the junk
in a plastic bag and then pulling it back up on a string
after customs. Nuts! But Apple figures it out and
writes it up."

"Makes himself a few enemies."

"Yeah, yeah." Moses seemed cheered at the
thought. "That's true. Billy didn't tend to care who he
dragged out in the sun."

"But you don't think it was dopers killed him."

"He came to see me one day. Said he had a new
story idea, and it was *me.*" Moses's eyes gleamed and
showed Gun years of wishing. "He ask me how come I
always miss the Hall of Fame, and I told him it's old
Ferdie Millevich. You know this, Gun: You don't have
to kill nobody to be guilty. People see your face next to
a headline with Grand Jury in it, it's like they're
seeing a mug shot. That's why I never make the Hall, I
told Billy."

The coffee was strong and better than what Gun
brewed in his fish house. It hummed and put a fine
alertness just behind the eyes, where it counted.
"Billy," Gun said, "decided to exhume the Millevich
case."

Moses nodded. "He said it needed clearing up. For

12

good. The coroner called it suicide, but it took him a week to do it, and who listened?"

"You mean Billy wanted to clear you. For something you never even went on trial for."

"He thought it might help. Come Hall of Fame voting."

Gun was quiet, sifting it down. It made some sense.

"I was his hero when he was a kid. A lot of people have said that to me, Gun. He was the first one who ever did anything with it."

There was a sudden need for sleep, or breakfast. Moses provided eggs and enough cheese for a modest omelette, and also Cap'n Crunch Peanut Butter Cereal and whole milk getting ready to sour. And more coffee. They finished at sunup.

"How'd it go with the cops?" Gun said. He felt fresh enough to be curious again.

"Fine. It helped that the kid who handled me grew up in Minnesota. Another *fan.*" Moses smiled. "He wanted to know where I was when Billy got killed. I said, I was with a woman. He took my statement and sent me home."

"They have any ideas?"

"Not ones I know about. They've kept a pretty good lid on it so far, too. No press. I turned my phone off, though, for when it gets out, probably this morning." Moses went abruptly silent. For the first time Gun noticed the changes in his face, the folds of skin on the eyelids, the two-day brush of whiskers white now across his chin.

"You want to tell me what happened?"

The chin settled down closer to the chest. "I was asleep on the pull-out there, it was maybe one in the morning. This lady's with me, woman I saw a lot of for a while but not really no more, and first thing I know she's shovin' me awake sayin', 'Answer the phone, hey.' I sleep heavy, see. But it's Billy, saying he's at the

13

airport, just got in, he's all thrilled about something. It's the big break on the Moses Gates story, he says, can I meet him? I say damn right, ten minutes, and then he says wait—he's got to run out of town for something, he'll be back at his place in three hours, can I be there? He promises it'll be worth the four A.M. run. So I get up then and I'm going nuts here, Gun, I'm tellin' you. Pace the floor, lots of coffee, I'm thinking about my bronze in the Hall of Fame. Linda wanted to sleep but I dragged her out, poured some champagne. Even the damn dog got a beer."

"Where'd Billy go?"

"I don't know. I'm not thinking about his errands then, I'm thinking about getting out from under all the hangman crap's been on me for the last fifteen years. Anyhow at quarter to four out I go, driving fast, and I get to Billy's place, nice little spread, his car's out front. But nobody answers the door. It wasn't locked. What would you do? So in I go, and there's Billy in the living room, and the first thing I think is what's he standing on, up so high? Your mind quits on you, like. He's up against the chimney and sort of lit from below, see, from the fire. I almost think he's playing a joke until finally it hits that he's hanging, really and truly, he's as dead as he's ever gonna get."

"And then you called the cops."

"I tell you about the smell in there? Listen. When I walked in the first thing I heard was that big fire crackling, and then I breathe and it's like somebody laid a bad pig on the luau. Sweet and burnt. Billy's feet, you see, down by the fire . . . all bare and crispy. There were fingernail scrapes on his ankles where they'd yanked his socks off."

Gun got up and went to a small window looking east. The sun was turning the Intracoastal gold and white. "What do you think he found out? He say anything at all about his 'big break'?"

"Uh-uh. I don't even know what direction he was going." Moses poured himself the last of the coffee. "They turned his place over pretty good, I mention that?"

"What for?"

"The more you ask, the more I don't know. They really did it, though. Messed up paintings on the wall, pillows on the furniture all ripped up. They were looking for something."

"What, notes? He was a reporter."

"Yeah. Maybe." Moses squinted at nothing. "You think the Millevich thing got him killed somehow?"

"No idea. Guys like this Billy Apple, sounds like there are plenty of people might not like him. Let the cops figure it out. What is it?"

Moses was staring at him.

"Billy's notes," he said. "I know where he kept them." Moses got to his feet. "It's nothing fancy, no safe or anything, just a little panel behind the medicine cabinet. I was over there one night, he was interviewing me. He had this cognac he said he kept for his big stories . . . We drank too much of it and had some good lies and big laughs. Then all of a sudden he says, 'You wanna see a paranoid guy?' Well, sure. So he takes me in the can and pulls out the aspirin and Pepto-Bismol and there it is, a little piece of plastic comes right out the back of the cabinet. There's a hole in the Sheetrock back there. He says, 'Some of the pricks I write about, you've got to practice discretion.'"

"He have anything in there?"

"Naw, not then. It was weeks ago, though."

Gun reached in his pocket and rubbed the keys to the Chevy. "Did you mention the medicine cabinet to the cops?"

"Never thought of it. Too damn sorry."

"Can we get in and take a peek?"

Moses frowned and Gun knew he'd rather not go

back to Billy Apple's. Then he reached for the phone, slowly, and punched up a number.

"I'd like to speak to Sergeant Morrell, please," he said. "Tell him it's Moses Gates calling."

It was a short conversation. Morrell, the Minnesota boy, was about to go off duty. He didn't ask questions. He said he'd meet them at Apple's house in half an hour.

"Your faithful public." Gun grinned. "They never let you down."

Moses had splashed his face and brushed his teeth and was pulling a fresh T-shirt over his belly when somebody knocked, tentatively, as though afraid to disturb this early. Moses scowled at the clock and at Gun and the knock came again, two shy taps. Moses crossed to the door and opened it to empty air. Nobody. From inside Gun could see the splitting concrete sidewalk, brown dead grass, and the night-blue hood of the rented Beretta. Then Moses stepped out and had strong hands all over him, from right and left, and the hands picked him up and pitched him face-first on the hood of the car, and the shock took his wind so that he didn't resist or yell for Gun, though Gun came anyway.

4

There were four of them busy on Gates in the new sun and with the dog still squatting on the grass Gun went to work. The nearest was a dense meaty man who had Moses's left knee over the wheel well of the Beretta

and was slowly convincing it to bend *forward;* Gun
wrapped a hand around the man's forehead and pried
him back, swung back his own knee and buried it in a
fleshy kidney. The man dropped and crawled, face to
the ground like he was looking for his lost breath,
found it at last and screamed. It brought the attention
of the others. One of them, a lanky Hispanic with an
overconfident face, let go of Moses and looked up at
Gun unfazed. He said, *"Tall* mothah." He started for
Gun and another followed, a teenage white kid with
effeminate lips and a T-shirt that said YOU HUG YOU
DIE. Behind Gun the kidney man tried to sit up. The
dog moaned and crouched. The kid with the T-shirt
was coming straight in now with his face nervous
while the Hispanic angled in from the side. One guy
still had Moses, was lifting his head and smashing it
down into the Chevrolet, doing it again, again. The
white kid dove in and pulled Gun's mind from the
Hispanic who was right in there then and had a silver
thing in his hand. The silver thing arced and Gun saw
it close up, a socket wrench, *duck it duck it* but
six-feet-six doesn't duck easily and he twisted to catch
the wrench on the upper arm. The white kid had hold
like a damn Chihuahua now, clawing and clinging, not
biting yet but being one hell of an irritation and Gun
knew he had to take the Hispanic out or he'd lose this
one and hurt mightily when he woke up on the
sidewalk. He let the Chihuahua hang on his waist and
feinted for the Hispanic, then when the socket wrench
was out of range swung down and swept the white
kid's legs into the air. He held them before his face
shins-outward, the kid still gripping his waist upside
down and gasping with the effort of it. The Hispanic
let go of his smile and got both hands on the grip of the
wrench. He faked moves left, right, came in straight
and swung for the head the way Gun needed him to
for this to go easy. Gun tightened his hold on the
Chihuahua's legs and offered them up to the wrench,

17

which had enough speed to splinter both shinbones and turn the kid into thick jelly. The Hispanic saw his buddy go into shock and swing loosely from Gun's grip, said, "Ahh, dahmn the lady," and tucked the wrench into his acid-washed jeans while backing away toward the Intracoastal. In his corner sight Gun saw Moses still facedown on the Beretta. The big blond-haired guy was done pounding him now and was bent down with a hand on Moses's neck, talking earnestly into his ear. Gun saw Moses nod twice, his nose rubbing metal. He laid the kid with some gentleness on the brown grass next to the dog, who came over to sniff, then started for the car and got surprised again when Moses's left arm came to life. The catcher's paw at the end of it rose up wide and strong and found a hank of blond hair. Leverage enough. Gun saw the muscles move in that left arm and the blond man's face twist and go down hard against the windshield. Moses braced and pushed himself upright, very ugly in the face just now, and took a new grip against which the blond man wiggled.

Gun said, "Can we wait a minute, here?"

Moses was panting with the stress of the unexpect-edly battered. "Not gonna wait no minute." He fumbled with the man's head for a second and raised him upright. Gun realized Moses had him by both ears and was shaking him hard. "Ought to tear them straight offa your *skull,*" Moses shouted.

Behind Gun the kidney man at last stood up successfully and started a cramped quiet walk toward the sea. The kid with unlucky shins was awake and had the whimpers. The dog gave a sudden, joyous yip and started scratching up earth with its back feet.

Now that Moses had the blond man's ears he was communicating furiously. "So you her cute-ass little *boyfriend,* what do you, *own* the woman? Hey? She come back to me because she's missin' something with you maybe? *Boyfriend?"*

Well, it was the usual thing then. Gun felt hollow at having wrecked a man's legs over nothing more than someone else's woman trouble. He called, "Say, Moses, take a stretch, will you?" He walked slowly to the still-open door of the Gates Motel and sat down on the threshold. The adrenaline was going fast now and taking with it the interest and caffeine he'd used instead of sleep. He felt like he was back on the plane with Mrs. New York hearing three hours of narration about her sister. Wanting to avoid this he stood up again. He went to the kid, whose pants were soaking up blood now over the shins and whose womanlike lips were gray and murmuring, though admirably quiet. He picked the kid up as easily as he could and carried him past Moses, who still had hold of the man's ears and seemed to be settling in for the day, to a long yellow Lincoln Continental. It was early '80s and had a flattened roll of rubber-backed carpet across the backseat.

"You get here in this?" Gun said.

The kid nodded. Gun opened the back door and laid him in on the roll of carpet. On the back of the tan leather seat someone had printed YOU DON'T SMOKE JACKASS in black marker.

"I know this won't help," Gun said, "but I feel bad, about the legs. Your buddy's socket wrench, I had to grab something. It wasn't worth it. For either of us."

It didn't help. Gun listened but the kid didn't open his mouth, so he shut the car door and went to Moses and tapped him on the shoulder. He said, "Don't hurt Blondie too much."

Blondie had his hands over Moses's hands over his ears. His eyes were as wild as a pig's at slaughter.

"Why in the hell not?" Moses gave a shake.

"He's got to drive his little pal to the hospital. And himself, it looks like."

Finally Moses let go, the storm leaving him and dissipating into the slow seaside breeze of this fine morning. Blondie put his hands to his ears tenderly and not finding the words to leave, went to the Lincoln in silence. The car rumbled, backed out of its spot, and coughed its way out of their hearing.

The sun was only a little higher over the ocean. Across the highway a swirl of gulls screamed and dipped. The kid's legs bothered Gun and he thought a broad repentance. Then the good salt heat flooded him and he tore up a handful of grass to rub blood from his fingers.

Moses had taken off his shirt and was wiping blood from his face. In one of the motel windows a tiny black girl watched, crying. Moses said, "We get cleaned up, we can still head over to Billy's."

The dog had trotted up gladly to Gun and he reached down to scratch it. He said, "You catchers sure do take a beating."

5

In the car Gun said, "Did you know this woman was so popular?"

They were going north on the Intracoastal Highway with the wind rising off the Atlantic almost too cool for lowered windows.

"No big shock. Linda never had a hard time finding company." Moses's face after a wash didn't look so bad, a couple short deep cuts on the cheeks, a place on the forehead like a bad rash. A little puffier than normal. "When she showed up that evening I hadn't seen her in half a year. Hadn't realized how sick of my own self I was until I saw her. She came in and I thought, I'm a sad piece of crap, but not no more."

"That was the night Billy died."

Moses nodded once. "She wouldn'ta stayed long, though, Billy or not."

The fight had been nasty for the Beretta. There was a long shallow dent in the center of the hood where Moses had landed, and a smaller sharp pock Blondie had hammered in using Moses's head. It was a topographical disaster. Now Gun turned the bruised Chevy left on Arlington Road and steered past small farms interspersed with roadside fruit stands, still vacant in the morning, their long windows covered with sheets of plywood.

"Left again," said Moses, and they turned in at one of the fruit shacks that was minus plywood, paint, or fruit. A dirt track led behind the shack and into a small grove of mature citrus trees. Orange and grapefruit, mixed, the fruit hanging from boughs in nearly ripe corpulence. The heavy scent made Gun feel strong and slightly off balance, as though he were breathing pure vitamin C.

"Private orchard," Moses said. "Billy'd just bought the place. Old fella had it before used to pick all his fruit himself and sell it out his roadside window. Hobby. Billy talked about doing the same thing. Some days he got sick of newspapering."

The track led over a hummock where the fruit trees stood off to let in some sun, and topping it they saw the weathered home of Billy Apple. An old house of unpainted Florida cypress, bigger than it looked at first: two stories topped by a steep roofline that leveled down in front over a generous southern porch, blooming azaleas rushing up under a set of paned windows on the west side, other greenery in full wildness pressing in on the place as if coveting the ground it was built on. A yellow police ribbon was taped around the house and tied off in front with something like a Christmas bow. The porch held a swaybacked davenport, and the davenport held Sergeant Morrell.

"Mr. Gates," he said, standing as the car rolled up. He was a tall one, made taller by gauntness and the uniform and somehow by the spare crop of mustache hairs riding his upper lip. He was clutching his pointy policeman's cap in both hands. "And Mr. Gun Pedersen. I'll be damned, it's the All-Star team." Morrell was grinning. "Thought you were gonna stand me up. Say, Mr. Gates, you get hit or something?"

"Just another jealous boyfriend. You know how it goes."

"Sure I do, ha-ha." Morrell grinned some more. Even his teeth were tall and thin.

They ducked under the awkwardness of the police tape and shook hands. Gun said, "So you're in charge of the Apple investigation."

"Nope. I'll be helping out with it, though." Morrell looked uncomfortable. "It's gotta be confidential, me letting you come here this way. You see? My superiors wouldn't understand, Mr. Pedersen."

"Gun."

Most of the worry left Morrell's face, but not all. "So do you fellows just want to see the place, or is it something in particular?"

Moses explained about the cubbyhole. "We just thought it was worth a look. If they wanted his notes . . ."

Morrell was back to grinning as he produced a key and snapped it in the lock. "Say, I know you feel some responsibility here, Moses—"

"Mr. Gates."

"—since he *was* doing a story about you and everything, but you understand that Apple had his fingers in a lot of different, ah, pies." The darkened house as they stepped inside smelled of stale smoke and old food, milk going bad in the refrigerator. Morrell didn't appear to notice. "He did some really dangerous stuff, made some genuine bad people very mad. Remember that coke piece he did, the South American soccer guys?"

"Mm-hmm."

"Well, that story popped a pretty big pipeline, real men's-club stuff. You think the old boys were some kinda pissed off? You bet." He smiled down upon Gates with the look that people who know give those who don't. "That was Apple's habit, pissing people off. I used to read him all the time. He had fun with it."

Gun was quiet. The half-dark house made hollow settling sounds. Moses said, "He didn't have so damn much fun here the other night."

"Mr. Gates, you told me right off Billy Apple was an old fan of yours. That's why he was looking into all that business with Ferdie Millevich, right? To show everybody once and for all you were in the clear. To get you in the Hall of Fame." Morrell's voice went gentle. "Geez, Mr. Gates, I'm a fan of yours, too. It's a shame now Billy can't finish what he was doing. But that was a lot of years ago. It's history, is what it is. I don't know . . . history's not something people get killed for, generally."

Morrell added the "generally" to appease Moses, Gun knew. He said, "We'd like to have a look in the bathroom, anyhow."

"Sure. Sure. You just don't ever know." Morrell seemed glad to get moving again and led them to the right, past the sour kitchen to the bathroom.

There was a moment as the young cop took down aspirin bottles and ruinous disposable razors when Gun heard Moses's breath quicken, and then they had the cubbyhole open. It was maybe a foot square, framed by pine two-by-fours, and bare as a blown egg.

"Say, nice little spot, though," Morrell said, over-full of solace. "There *would* be plenty of room for a notebook in here." He craned his long neck as though looking closely might show something after all in the hole. "You know," he said, "we never did find many notes of his. The newspaper office told us he worked out of his home most of the time, and we did find a few things—scrapbooks and some shorthand junk, nothing current. We figure he was one of those guys, he kept most of his working stuff on computer."

"Here?"

"Yeah. Lousy break for us, after they killed Apple they went over the whole house pretty well. Used a tire wrench or something on all his machinery. Smashed up his television, VCR, his stereo stack. And a computer, a Macintosh, wouldn't you know it? We got it pretty much cleaned up now. You want to see the rest of the place?"

It was a little brighter now, the sun just getting in over the nearest orange trees and showing them rooms despoiled: Impressionist prints razored and sagging in their frames, chairs tipped forward, their backs and bottoms opened, showing guts. Around it all was the haphazard order left by investigation; a heavy wooden-shafted reading lamp, lifted and inspected and placed back down off center.

"Sergeant," Moses said, "Billy told me he really had something with all this Ferdie Millevich business. Maybe he'd figured something out they couldn't afford for him to write about."

"Could be." Morrell sighed. "Could be he'd learned something real mysterious and they killed him to shut him up and then scoured the place and got his notes so nobody'd ever find out what it was. Yeah, it's all possible. But I got to tell you guys, R-rated thrillers aside, people usually don't get killed so they *won't* do something. They get killed for *doing* it."

A moment of quiet.

"You think it was revenge for some story he did?"

"Look at how he died, yeah, it seems that way." Morrell looked at Gun. "Mr. Gates tell you about his feet? Not that Billy felt any pain. The fire was a little extra hate, was all."

"What were they looking for?" Gun nodded at a slashed chair.

"You tell me. Maybe Billy took a payoff and they wanted it back. I'll be honest with you, we don't have shit."

Morrell saved the living room for the final flourish, leading them in with a cathedral hush. It was smaller than Gun had imagined, ruled by the fieldstone fireplace facing the door, and barely furnished with a straight-backed oak rocker and a slender writing table and chair. The room, though small, had been left open all the way to the peaked second-story ceiling. A single pane of glass high on the southern exposure sent a slanting column of light to the red carpet. It would have been, Gun thought, like dying in a chapel.

"The rope was tied up there." Morrell pointed to a place on the chimney halfway up where there were unmortared gaps between the stones. "That's the draft for the fireplace. Guy pulled that little table over to stand on, getting the rope through those chinks. We found the marks from the table legs on the rug."

There were several chalky burned-out bits of log in the rack. On the stone hearth Gun could see dried dime-size spatters, like drippings from a black candle. For Moses he said, "Morrell, Billy Apple was investigating the death of a man who died by hanging. Now he's dead, of hanging. That must be worth looking into."

Morrell had been dangling his policeman's cap from the middle finger of his right hand. Now he tucked it firmly onto his head with the brim at his eyebrows. "Mr. Pedersen, we're looking into it. We're looking into every damn corner of this thing, and we're going to keep doing it until we get"—he looked

25

at Moses—"the *real* hangman. But listen. What happened to Billy Apple, he got himself hanged. What happened to Ferdie Millevich, go look it up if you want to, he hanged him*self.* Now you show me the similarity."

Gun looked at it from the neck down and saw that there was none, and nodding to Moses they followed the sergeant out into hard sun and orange-tasting air.

6

There was no talk on the drive back to the motel where they now sat, still in the Chevy with the engine running, windows up, air-conditioning on.

"Anybody dies in this idiot state, they blame it on the drug dealers," Moses said. "You hear that Morrell? Talking about the damn coke pipeline and the South Americans. Just one time I wish they'd give the drug dealers the day off, get back to the rest of us."

"He didn't take the Ferdie thing too seriously," Gun agreed. "Why don't you get out now, go mind your motel. Got a game this afternoon?"

"One-fifteen, West Palm Park. Where you headed?"

"Out looking. Maybe Billy's pals at the newspaper know more than they told the cops."

Moses smiled, his lips pushing the new bruises into shiny knobs. "What are you, Travis McGee?"

"Sorry," Gun said. "You're not pretty enough."

The *By-Line* was not the dominant newspaper of West Palm Beach. It didn't have a million readers or machines all over the city like the *Post* or that foolish national jokes-and-graphics rag. What it did have was a nice location, one block off the ocean in a small square office complex just high enough to see over the red tile roof of the mansion between itself and the Atlantic. Gun wondered how such an unpretentious brown structure had ever been built here, on such plainly envied ground. It violated what he'd noticed about the city's unwritten code: on the seaside, private mansions. First block in, financial institutions, about one per mansion in the clean white stone of money-changers' preference. More white stone another block inland, this headlined in simple neon with the names of dress designers and art dealers. Beyond, the wilderness: schools the same as schools anywhere, cheap T-shirt stores, ballparks, fish shops on streets the city hadn't swept in years. Coming in on the low side Gun had seen a scrawny raccoon pawing through the gutter's urban humus. The Everglades.

Looking without success for parking he ended up a little off the money district and put the Chevy in a lot next to a boarded-up theater. Across the lot a stadium's lights rose above palm trees. A marquee told tourists this was West Palm Park: OLD BALL IS GOOD BALL, CHEER OUR PATRIARCHS. Gun locked the Beretta and aimed for the sea.

A block from the *By-Line* he passed a pin-striped old man in a motorized wheelchair. From behind, the man's head seemed to lean back in first one direction, then another; there was an irritating *humm* Gun thought came from the chair itself, but catching the old man and going by him he saw it was something else.

The man, out for a drive in his Sunday suit, was shaving.

With an electric razor, a pricey one, pointing his chin here and there, getting at the rough spots.

Gun smiled, saw the old man's eyes only mildly

distracted, went on ahead. Then a voice soft but somehow sharp pierced the hum of the razor.

"Gun Pedersen. Stop a moment, please."

Turning, Gun saw the old man had halted his chair and had him by the eyes. He was making a few final cleanup sweeps down close to his shirt collar, which was drawn tight by a deep red paisley tie. He shut off the thing at last and said, "It's my unfortunate lot not to have your card with me today."

There were days it was not handy to have to admit who you were. Many days. "Card?" Gun asked.

"You despise this. I completely understand," the man said. He had on a pair of black-rimmed drugstore glasses, the bows tilted upward until they gripped his head an inch above the ears. The lenses angled so sharply the world must have seemed a continuous down slope. "However, now that I have you, on a very public street, the conventions of courtesy leave you little choice. I'll have your autograph now, thank you."

The old man produced a Bic from his breast pocket and a folded sheet of paper from under the suit coat. On the sidewalk people passed them quickly, their attention conspicuously elsewhere. Gun signed.

"Efficient, aren't you?"

"What I am," the old man said, studying Gun's signature, "is a detached old bastard, a decrepit and heinous collector of artifacts. Baseball in particular," he said, his eyes meeting Gun's with a calm brilliance, "to a dangerous degree."

Gun grinned naturally at this but there was no grinning left in the old man and so he stopped and said instead, "You work this corner much?"

"I work nothing. Things come to me." He bent forward in the chair, which was upholstered in red paisley to match the tie. Maybe, Gun thought, he owned other wheelchairs: Tartan plaid, Oxford stripes, Little Eddie Bauer ducks.

"You'll see, Pedersen, that I don't much care for a simple scrawl on twenty-pound bond. In your case it'll have to do; as I told you, I'm unprepared. See." The old man had reached beneath the seat as he spoke and brought up a slender case of glowing black wood the size of a box of Havanas. He laid it on his lap and opened the lid with the careful fingers of a curator. Within were baseball cards.

"A small collection, carefully chosen for the day," he said.

"I see."

"I'm quite certain that you don't. Of the several hundred, let's say, past-prime ballplayers attempting to get it all back in this—" he smiled his disgust— "*Senior* League, there are a few dozen who used to own considerable talent."

"Once upon a time."

"Yes. Of those, there are still at least half a dozen whose messy signatures I've not got." He showed a scant handful of plastic-encased cards, men with bats on their shoulders smiling at a point over the camera. Gun knew most of them. "I get them to sign their cards, the cards from their best years. Some of these fellows, now, are playing for the local old-fart contingent; the others for the group out of Tallahassee, which will play our *boys* this afternoon. Batting practice begins in less than two hours."

"Ought to afford a few scalps," Gun said.

The old man broke into a giggle at that and giggled for some moments, literalizing the remark in his head. "Ought to indeed." He chuckled. Getting control again he said, "Your being here surprises me, Pedersen. You don't seem the type to be riding the nostalgia barge. If I'd known you were on the roster I'd have been ready with your card."

"Not playing. I'm just here seeing an old friend. So you'll have to be happy with your twenty-pound bond."

The black box was stowed again and Gun was glad of it somehow. It gave him an uneasiness he couldn't quite place.

"Of course," the old man said, "you may run across me again. I'll try to be carrying next time. There's so much more *spiritual* value to the cards." He had the chair started again and Gun walked next to him until they reached the *By-Line*.

"I get off here," said Gun.

The old man spun his chair to face Gun straight on, peered up cynically through his black-framed glasses. "An old friend, you say? Tell me, and who might this be?"

"Moses Gates."

"Ah, Mr. Gates." Nodding, eyes closed for a moment. Then shaking his head the way grown-ups do when amused at children. "Coming to help the poor man out, I imagine, set things right. Restore lost honor."

Gun looked at the man for a moment, thinking, *You've sure got it all figured.* "When did you hear about the murder?" Gun asked.

"Me? Why yesterday, of course. I have friends everywhere. It's my attractive personality"—he looked off in the distance, squinted—"and the pity helps, too." He slapped the arms of his chair and turned his eyes back toward Gun. "What a marvelous emotion, pity." He laughed. "Sincerely now, Mr. Pedersen, I am glad you're here."

"Why's that?" Gun asked.

The man looked down at his lap and carefully smoothed out his red paisley tie between his index and middle fingers. "Unlike you," he said, "I have no particular interest in Moses Gates, but I must say it is quite difficult for me to think of the man as a killer. I'm sure you agree?"

Gun did, and said so.

"Well." The old man moved his hand to the controls, and his chair came to life. "Good-bye, Mr. Pedersen." He nodded his head and began to roll away down the walk. "Your finest season," Gun heard him say, "was 1968. Three thirty-nine, forty-four homeruns, one hundred twenty-six RBIs. World Series MVP."

Gun stood blinking at the retreating wheelchair.

"Hold onto your hair," the old man called.

7

Among the things the *By-Line* didn't have, along with Billy Apple anymore, were a sense of order and a receptionist. A sign in the lobby had directed Gun to the top floor and when he stepped off the elevator it was to an empty hall and the smell of new paint. The hall led past several doors with bumpy-glassed windows that showed Gun light but nothing else. Finally, a door with lettering: NEWS, CITY.

He went in and saw a room the size of a basketball court only squashed shorter by an artificial ceiling abundant with fluorescent tubes. Under the tubes people labored in cubicles, hunched toward computer screens. From Gun's height it looked mazelike, a newsroom designed to confound white mice. There were several real offices around the perimeter, offices with real walls and real windows. Behind one window a man and a woman stood speaking, the woman facing out over the maze. She had pale perfect skin and a tight knot of hair fighting gray and was talking, talking fast. Gun told himself to stop watching, *it's an argument, let them have it themselves,* but it was hard to look away, Lord, the chilly way her lips moved. The man was a big one, his back to Gun, hands clasped behind his head, thumbs massaging his neck under the lapel of an expensive suit coat. Rubbing hard while the woman talked on. Looked like a man who was losing, Gun thought, and then the guy half turned and Gun recognized him like a picture from a high school yearbook.

Harold Ibbins. Didn't go back as far as high school but it almost seemed like it, those early years playing ball. Ibbins had been one of those guys he passed on the way to the majors, not a natural but a hard worker who'd gotten there finally and done utility jobs around the American League, mostly with the Twins until he had a hot streak and Griffith traded him. Nice enough guy, as Gun remembered him, though Moses swore Ibbins had once driven over the foot of a teammate "so he could get some innings. His agent told him to do it."

Ibbins turned almost enough to catch Gun looking. Gun stepped back through the newsroom door and down the hall to the elevator, where he stood pretending concern over the directory on the wall.

Copy Room	403
Janitorial	405
City News	409-11

Well. Ought to have noticed that before. Gun looked it over another time before a door whined open down the hall and here came Harold, walking slow, one hand still rubbing his neck.

Gun turned and let his eyebrows go up. "Harold Ibbins. What'd you do, go newspaper on us?"

Harold had always had a grin. It arrived now,

though the eyes above it were preoccupied. "Gun. Nope, me and the media don't share the same shower, no more than we have to. Now especially, I'm here to tell you." The grin fading, joining the eyes.

"Why's that?"

Harold kneaded his neck. "Aw, hell, Gun. These incompetent"—his eyes came suddenly sharp— "papers these days can't print an ad right if you draw it for 'em in the sand."

"Screwed up your copy, hey?"

Something in Gun's voice made Harold hesitate. "Yeah." He reached for the elevator button. "I'm in the land business now, Gun. You think: real estate, Florida, man's doing *fine,* and I am. But hell, it's still retail; you still got to advertise." Close up his face showed capillaries the color of red wine.

Gun pointed down toward the newsroom. "Hope you reamed 'em out good."

"Like an ump in hell," Harold said. His eyes met Gun's again and looked relieved when the elevator bell rang. "Adios," he said, and it wasn't until the doors were closed and Harold was sinking through the building that Gun smelled the man's sweat on the air.

He stepped into the newsroom and she came toward him like Harold had just been the warm-up match. Khaki suit, he noticed now, and a don't-waste-my-time stride.

"Taylor Johns," she said. The voice matched the walk. "City editor. Is there something I can do for you?"

"Maybe. Were you Billy Apple's boss?"

The stare she gave Gun made his neck muscles go tight. He thought of Harold, kneading. She said, "What, are you guys standing in line? Who's next?" She craned angrily, looking past him.

"If we could talk," he said.

She led him through the maze of cubicles and low

phone whispers and clicking keyboards to one of the real offices. It was on the good side of the building. Gun recognized the red tiles of the neighboring mansion and beyond it the ocean. She closed the door and pointed to a chair of some kind of black Saran Wrap and he sat with trepidation.

"I was his boss," she told him, "though he never seemed to think so. Maybe I didn't either." She looked at Gun and he saw some hope there, under the ice.

"I'm sorry about Billy."

"I only heard last night," she said. "A few people here still don't know. I haven't had the strength."

Taylor Johns, Gun thought, looked like a woman who would have the strength.

"Billy was our boy," she said.

He let enough quiet pass to show respect and when she looked up, expectant, he said, "I'm here because of a story he was working on. A piece about Moses Gates, a ballplayer—"

"Moses Gates, the wrongly faulted man, wishes to reclaim place in the sun," she said. Laying it out like that and sounding sick of it. "Never makes the Hall of Fame because too many people still blame him for teammates's death . . . that the piece?"

"Right. It was Moses Gates who found Billy."

"Good for Moses. And you, you're Gun Pedersen, I know you now. Friend of Gates, I suppose."

"Yes."

"Certainly. And you're here because Billy interviewed you, and now you're having second thoughts about being named as a source in the story. My advice, Mr. Pedersen, is not to worry. Billy never finished that story, or the box of others he had in the works. You needn't fear." She said it so fast that he could only sit in the plastic chair thinking, *How can she talk that way? Like her lips are frozen.* Poor nervous Harold, he hadn't had a prayer.

He held up a hand. "I never talked to Billy. Was that what Ibbins was after?"

"Ibbins?"

"Tall guy, suit coat. You just talked to him."

"Harry, he said. Yes. Came in saying he'd been interviewed and then had changed his little mind about being on the record. Told me more about the Gates piece than I'd ever heard from Billy. Wanted us to cut the story, not that it matters now."

"He didn't know about Billy?"

"Seemed not to."

Gun remembered Harold's sweat and the way his finger shook pressing the elevator button as if from drink or fear. "Does Harold run his realty ads in this paper?"

"Ads?" Her mouth looked like it had found a bad taste. "Don't ask me about ads. Ads are two floors down. Why are you here, Mr. Pedersen?"

"Moses Gates is an old friend of mine. He thinks Billy was killed because of the story he was working on."

She eyed him sadly, almost with pity. "Well of course he was," she said. "It was always a story, the boy had nothing else. But Mr. Pedersen, which story? The blessing of Billy was that he could do anything, and he did, all at once. He was everyone's buddy, everyone gave him tips, everyone was a contact. He always had a dozen stories in the hopper, or three dozen."

"Moses thinks it was the baseball story."

She sighed and turned from mother to editor.

"All right. Why?"

"Well, because Billy called him at home that night. He was excited, wanted to see Moses. Only when Moses got there . . ."

"Mr. Pedersen, I can see how it looks to you. But the Moses Gates story was something Billy was doing, well, from the heart. He was sick of writing stuff about drugs and guns and wanted to do something that had some sweetness to it." She turned her eyes on Gun and they were getting soft again. "Did you ever see a silly movie about two guys, they dressed in black suits, wore sunglasses, drove around the country putting their old rock group back together? They kept saying they were on a mission from God."

"Yeah."

Taylor Johns shook her head. "Billy was that way. He could go out and do the big important story and get praised to the skies, but he really lived for the sweet stories, the ones he *felt.* He wanted Moses Gates to get into the Hall of Fame. No danger there, just a little harmless crusading. Billy was always on a mission from God."

"He didn't tell you what he had on the baseball piece? Who he was talking to, what direction he was taking?"

"He didn't tell me *squat* about what he was doing," Taylor said, with the intermittent bitterness of the bereaved. "Not a damn thing! Most days he didn't even come in. He was home writing or out talking, playing the deep-cover man. Half the stuff he wrote, I wouldn't have approved it if he'd told me."

"Like the South Americans," Gun said.

"Sure, the South Americans. *And* the point shaving at the U, *and* that mobster business, when they tried to buy the Dolphins. I told him, 'You don't have to be Jack Anderson, okay?' It gets dangerous. But he'd get a wild hair, and besides his stuff always turned out so good. I didn't rein him in."

Gun thought he felt the plastic chair sinking under him and so he stood up. "Who did he talk to? Here, I mean. Was there someone he might've talked to about the baseball story?"

"I hired Billy. I taught him newswriting and moved

him up the ladder to columnist. When he wanted to
say something, he said it to me."

"Could I see his office?"

She stood, smiled wearily, spread her arms. "You're
in it," she said. "The police were through, of course.
Look around."

He looked, with Taylor Johns resigned and watching
from a corner, her graying twist beginning to unravel.
The office surprised him; it was so empty Gun had
assumed it wasn't being used, though it must have
been coveted by the white mice out there in the maze.
The desk was bare except for an electric typewriter
and a tan phone whose cord ran nakedly over the floor
to the wall. There were no photos of family, no framed
journalism awards, no Far Side cartoons taped up
anywhere.

"The cops cleared everything out, or what?"

"No. Billy didn't keep office hours. It's like I told
you: He liked to work at home. Sitting in the dark at
night, talking into his machine."

There was nothing else but a steel four-drawer filing
cabinet stuffed with old story clippings and too much
thick paper addressing William E. Apple's company
retirement plan. He shoved and the drawers rolled
shut long and cool and solid like the drawers in a
morgue.

"What about family," he said, smelling her exhaustion now, not wanting to push.

"He didn't talk about them much. His folks were
from Florida, Orlando I think, they divorced when he
was little. It was his older sister he was close to,
Diane. They lived with the mother and the dad went
up east someplace. Diane moved up there, too, after
her schooling. I think she's still up there."

"Up where?" he asked, but Taylor was away somewhere, chin high, one hand dreamily searching a
pocket of the khaki suit. He excused himself and she
was back suddenly, apologetic.

37

"I don't remember . . . New York or Baltimore, Boston. Bad news will find you, wherever," she said. Her hand came up out of the pocket holding a peach-colored tissue. She twisted it around a finger and dabbed her eyes.

"See now, it's starting," she said.

8

Twelve-thirty P.M.

Ballparks like this one made Gun happier than he had a right to be, even put him in a mood sometimes that made him question whether he'd done right by himself, leaving the game as he had. Today the sky was untouched by clouds, as clear and blue as an ocean from the window of a jet, and beneath it the well-tended grass of the field was so bright Gun's eyes hurt to look at it. From the highest row above third base he looked at the neat concrete shell surrounding the infield. No upper deck here, unless you counted the press box, and all the seats good ones, same cheap price, two and a half bucks. There was room for five, maybe six thousand, enough people for some noise but not so many you forgot what you came for.

Gun turned around and saw that Moses Gates was still trapped outside the park near the ticket booths. Reporters had blocked his path to the locker room and, amazingly, Moses seemed to be handling them just fine. He wasn't even trying to cut through the crowd, but just stood there, hands behind his back, answering questions, his head nodding once in a while. *Friend, it's going to get old fast,* Gun thought.

When the home team started taking their swings in the cage and the sun rose to its most damaging height, Gun walked down to the concession stand and bought an orange Patriarchs' hat with a green P on it, then took a seat behind the third-base dugout where he could stretch his legs a little. He knew the park well. During seventeen springs he'd played his share of games here. In his last one—it would have been 1980—he'd hit a ball into the battery of lights high above the left-field wall. The home run hadn't counted in his own mind because it came off an arm whose name no one remembered anymore, a kid with good speed but no hop.

"Hey! Gun?" Even before turning, Gun matched the voice to a face, but when he saw it he was still surprised. Everything had gotten bigger, cheeks and chin and nose, and the extra flesh crowded in on his eyes.

"Rott," Gun said, offering his hand. The man took it and shook vigorously. "You put on weight, Rott."

"Don't look so good yourself. What happened to your hair? The cold turn it white? Damn, it's good to see you!" Rott straightened his body self-consciously and sucked his belly in. He was jammed into a uniform that said Tallahassee Toucans across the chest, and he looked at Gun through those same small milky blue eyes you could never quite lock onto. Hard to know, hard to not like.

"Understand you're a boss man now," Gun said. "Good club, too, I hear."

Rott Weiler smiled, pointed to the team's name on his jersey. "Hootin' right, and we're the best you'll find in this horseshit league."

"Papers this morning tell me you're down a couple games to West Palm."

Rott took a snort of warm salt air and laughed, leaned forward confidentially and flicked his eyes in the direction of the parking lot. "You want to get technical, sure. But let's be honest, Gun. Old Moses's got one hell of a monkey on his back, and if I know him, he ain't smart enough to say uncle. He'll take his team right into the cellar with him. I mean, look at his guys right now"—Rott pointed at the field—"look at 'em, dragging their asses like a bunch of widows. *They* read the papers, too, they know what's coming. Believe me, West Palm's all done for the season."

"You never lacked for confidence," Gun said, "and I admire that, but I don't guess you're an expert on Moses Gates."

"Hey, don't get me wrong. I hope Gates ain't the guy they're sayin' he is. I hope to God he's innocent, just like you do, but you've gotta admit, things look real funny, this writer getting strung up like Ferdie was. Hell, though, guilty or not, I know one thing. If it's *me* in his position—shit going on in my life—I'm gonna clear out of the clubhouse for the sake of the team. How about you?" Rott's eyes quickened out of their haze for an instant, glimmered. Gun didn't answer, just looked at him. Rott shook his head, wincing a little. "I didn't mean it personally, Gun."

Gun let the silence swell up, then said, "Tell me. What's in it for you down here? Not the money, I wouldn't think." Rott's playing career had ended prematurely, bad back, and because of a smart agent, the Phillies had been forced to eat his big contract. At least a couple million, if Gun had it right. "A summer job up north?" Gun asked.

Rott smiled. "Could be. Tell you what—I've got this little place west of here not too far. Come on out for dinner tonight, we can talk. Catch up on the old days, sample the bullshit. How about it?"

Out the corner of his eye Gun saw Moses Gates

walking onto the field, shoulders all hunched up. "I might do that," he said.

Rott followed Gun's eyes to the field. "Hell, bring old Moses along."

From the infield grass Moses waved at Gun, then motioned toward the batting cage. A pitcher Gun recognized was standing on the mound back of the safety net, rubbing down baseballs. "We'll talk later, then," Gun said to Rott. "I think somebody wants me to try out the wood."

"Gun. I admire you, coming down to hold Mo's hand in his time of tribulation, but you want to use your head. God, I hate to see friends get hurt."

"Me, too." Gun left him and walked down onto the field. He saw Moses coming toward him talking and grinning at the same time and then over Moses's left shoulder another face he knew. Harold Ibbins, sitting just over the first-base dugout, a Patriarchs' hat on his head. Gripping a plastic-cup of beer, tapping it on his knee. Harold was scanning the field, and when his eyes got to Gun they held for a moment and passed on, though Gun raised a hand.

Gun needed to talk to Harold. Billy had, after all.

"So then," Moses was saying, "I take it you're gonna show me if you still got anything left in those wrists."

"Mmm."

"Go on now, I been waiting for this. Move your ass." Gates aimed toward home with a finger as big around as a bratwurst. Too many years catching heat.

In the dugout Gun chose a thirty-five-inch Hillerich and Bradsby with a narrow handle, same kind of tool he used against the pitching machine in his own backyard. He felt conspicuous, a little silly in his street clothes, like a Sunday fan pretending, but the bat was a natural presence in his hands and he walked

with it to the batting cage and watched the boys—
men, he reminded himself, old men—take their cuts.
Thirty-five was the minimum age in the new league.

Throwing was Hector Valdez, former Yankee relief
man, late innings mostly. He was a few years younger
than Gun, early to midforties now, and growing a
good paunch, but every time he let go of the ball it
found the strike zone. Hector was throwing easy, of
course, helping hitters find their eyes and rhythm, and
they slapped the ball to all fields: line drives, lazy flies,
wicked grounders. Fifteen minutes of this, hitters
taking their turns and Gun watching, then Moses
walked over from a pepper game and said, "Gun's up
now." The guy who was digging in stepped out of the
way.

On the mound, Hector went for the rosin bag. He'd
been eyeing Gun all along, showing nothing with his
face, but touching the long drooping points of his
mustache and every few minutes giving the smallest
flash of tooth. A couple times during Gun's years with
the Tigers he and Hector had squared off for real
stakes. Once with two gone in the ninth, an American
League championship at stake. Once during an All-
Star game. Gun beat him the first time, pulling a
double down the line and sending the game to extra
innings. The second time it was Hector's turn. Three
pitches, three whiffs.

He'd never been a finesse man, Hector. He leaned
back and threw smoke, nothing on the ball but Latin
emotion and a hell of a tail that came up and in on a
right-handed hitter. Hector's weakness had been control. Some days he was the pitching god, carving
corners like a chef carves a hundred-dollar rump.
Other days he couldn't find his own face in a mirror.
But good day or not, batters feared for their lives.

Gun wore a cotton T-shirt that gave him room to
swing, but stepping up to the plate he cursed his
trousers. They were too snug through the crotch and

waist, made him feel stiff and old. He knew of a few pounds he didn't need, exactly where they were and where he'd gotten them, and now he vowed to himself to be down to his playing weight—240 pounds—by the time he flew back home.

He filled his lungs and tapped the plate with the end of the bat. It didn't feel unnatural. With his Pony runners he dug notches in the packed dirt to support his wide stance. He cocked the bat behind his right ear and established his grip on the handle, not too tight. He did a small knee bend, snapped his right elbow against his rib cage. Lifted it, slowly. He was ready.

From the small dry smile on Hector's face Gun knew this was not going to be batting practice. He didn't smile back. *Okay, then, Hector, bring it.* He felt a wonderfully light, cool presence in the upper region of his gut, a buoyancy he'd never gotten past missing since his retirement ten years ago. Then Hector was into his motion.

The first pitch came so fast Gun could only pretend he had meant to take it. He tapped the plate again, nonchalant, let his eyes say, Try that again. The next one sailed two feet above his head. He stepped out of the box and took a swing to loosen his shoulders, then reached up and tapped his batting helmet, just to be sure it was there. He stepped back up to the plate.

He was ready for the third pitch, even had it timed right, but he swung through it, above or below he couldn't say. The count was one and two. No room for any more mistakes, and Gun liked it that way. He'd always done well, being forced to come from behind, and sometimes he wondered if he put himself there on purpose.

Hector stepped off the mound and picked up the rosin again from the rust-colored clay. He bounced it on his hand then tossed it down and hitched his pants up tight beneath his belly. Gun let the bat rest on his shoulder for a second and watched himself, on the screen inside his head, drive the next pitch over the left field wall. Instant replay in reverse. Hector, back on the rubber, let a full smile widen his face. Gun lifted the bat from his shoulder, prepared himself. Hector moved into his windup.

The pitch came in knee-high on the outside corner, perfect placement, and Gun felt his wrists snap at the instant of contact and the sudden release of compressed force, a shotgun minus the kick. Then Hector Valdez was on the ground, flat on his back, and the baseball whining into center field.

"You want a job, Gun? Free-lance Designated Hitter, whaddayou say?" Rott was standing behind the cage, pinching into a can of Red Man. "You look mean up there. Make the rest of these guys look over-the-hill."

"I don't need a job, Rott, and if I did it wouldn't be this. Not anymore. But thanks."

He tossed his bat toward the elderly batboy, who lifted a small fist and said, "Yeah!" then ran up and slapped Gun's back like he'd just busted up a game.

"He's not a baseball man," apologized Moses. "Lots of folks involved down here that aren't. Truth is, we're a sorry-ass league. Wait'll you see the game, you'll cry."

Gun didn't cry but felt like it. He went up behind first base thinking he'd talk to Harold during the game, but a fan told him the old utility man had left before his beer was even finished. Then play started and Gun went down to the Patriarchs' bench.

The level of skill wasn't the problem, though of course most of the players were a couple steps slower than they'd been. And the pitching wasn't bad, either, class double A, maybe. The problem had to do with soul. Nobody seemed to care a whole lot. They didn't run out their ground balls. Didn't bother to back up plays. They argued calls for show, laughing, Gun noticed, in the dugout afterward. It made him wonder why they'd come down here. The money wasn't much good, according to Moses, and most of the players were past big-league speed, without a prayer of showing the scouts what they wanted to see. But of course, it was still a show. Live crowd, kids wanting autographs, pretty girls in sports cars. Everything on a miniature scale, but all of it here nonetheless.

"What'd I tell you about Gates's team? They're finished." Gun was standing in the shade of a palm tree outside the rear entrance of the locker room, and Rott had come up behind him. He was sucking a beer and grinning. His team had won by a wide margin.

"Dull performance all around, if you ask me."

"It's not the bigs. Nobody said it was. But give my guys some credit; they knocked the shit out of the ball. You take 'em forty years old and give 'em a tenth of what they're used to making and what can a man expect?" Rott dropped to one knee and polished with his fingers the silver metal tips of his black cowboy boots. "Are you coming out tonight?" he asked.

Gun didn't know of any old times they had in common, but he'd decided a visit with Rott couldn't hurt, considering the man's strong opinions about Moses. "I think I will, thanks," he said.

Rott stood up and his eyes moved from Gun to the door of the locker room. "One thing, though. Maybe it's better you don't bring Moses along. He doesn't much like me. I make him nervous. You can imagine why."

Ten minutes later, as Gun and Moses left the park, the little autograph man was blocking the exit gate with his wheelchair. His narrow face was bright with cynical pleasure and his small hands, shuffling cards, looked as nimble as a monkey's. Gun and Moses left the sidewalk and vaulted the six-foot chain-link fence and ran to Moses's car. As they drove off, Gun took a peek backward and saw the Autograph Man waving his fist.

9

"Don't listen if you don't want to. I'm only telling you what I think, and I could be wrong. But let's face it, I probably know a little more about your friend than you do. I was on the man's team, remember, and I saw how it was between those two. People can think whatever they want about Ferdie getting himself offed, but to me it's not a real big mystery."

Rott was leaning forward, elbows propped on the marble lawn table, a long index finger cutting off every possibility of disagreement. Beyond a wide pasture of white horses was a tiny lake, bordered on one side by a clutch of mangroves.

Gun shrugged. When a man wanted to talk this bad you might as well let him talk.

"It's not a matter of having it out for anybody, Gun, or trying to prove myself right. But for the love of Judas, look at the facts. And then you got this alibi of his. You met that woman yet? I can't believe anybody's listening to her. And now *you're* down here, to set things right. Take it from an old friend, Gun. All you're doing is setting yourself up. I mean, open your eyes. What happens once you learn the stuff that other poor devil learned, that Billy what's-his-name. Hey, then *you* might swing."

"Other people don't see it that way. Other people that knew him then."

"Other people that knew him like *I* did? We roomed together, Gates and me. And I roomed with Ferdie, too. What other people? Let me tell you something about Moses. Something good. He's a guy that knows what loyalty means. Loyal like a dog, they say, and that's no putdown. There's another side to it though. When Ferdie comes along and leaks stuff to that Faust guy who writes for the paper, hey, Moses is never gonna forgive him for it. You understand? You don't go talking about your teammates behind their backs like Ferdie did. You just don't let him get by with that if your name is Moses Gates."

Gun finished his glass of orange juice, freshly squeezed and fortified, on ice. He stood up and turned a full circle, admiring the grounds.

Rott took the hint and stopped his tirade. "You like my little farm?" he asked.

"I like it very much. How many acres, did you say?"

"I've got three hundred here and another thirty along the ocean." He pointed to the east. "See that line of palmettos there? If you walk along it to the top of that rise you'd be able to see past the next guy's place to the water."

"And you say you built it yourself?" Gun nodded at the house, a southern plantation style with high front pillars and a wide double door of carved oak.

"Had it built, yeah."

"What year?"

Rott's eyes touched Gun's and moved away before answering. "Eighty-one. That's the year I moved down here."

"I didn't realize you got into that kind of money so young, Rott. You weren't more than what, twenty-six, twenty-seven then? Hadn't been in the majors for more than a couple years."

Rott motioned toward the house and followed Gun

inside. The room they entered was expansive, dark-stained wood flooring with light green Oriental rugs, furniture of Victorian design in natural tones, a wide marble fireplace on the far wall.

"Of course, the truth is, I didn't buy the place myself, or not all of it. You see, both my parents died in '80, and they left some money. Quite a bit." Rott led Gun across the room to the fireplace, on both sides of which hung large portraits of fierce-looking men in gray beards. One wore a Confederate officer's uniform, the other a black suit and hat.

"The soldier there's my great-grandfather. No, great-great. Dad's side. The other one, he's my mom's old man. Both Missourians. Serious bastards, you can tell. They'd be disappointed in me. Playing a stupid game, hanging their faces in Florida." Rott laughed, apparently pleased with himself, and pointed at the soldier. "He was a major and far as we can tell never did anything during the war to immortalize our name. Though he did show up at the Wilderness and get his ass shot up good. I'm supposed to resemble him, but never did see it myself. Probably the beard."

More than the beard, Gun thought. Try the eyes, the nose, and the shape of the head. "What about the businessman?" he asked.

"Oh, he did lots of things. Made lots of dough. Lost some, too. Mostly what he did was get lucky, though. He got into insurance in the late forties, sold a lot of it, then dumped it all into computers. So my folks had it pretty good, but died before they had a chance to enjoy it too much. My dad sold insurance, too, and just couldn't get around to retiring. Could have, but didn't. Had the work ethic of his old man. Not me though. Them things skip generations sometimes, is what they say."

"You said it, not me." Gun remembered the stories that circulated when Rott left the Phillies. Not a bad back so much as too little conditioning and too much food.

"A guy gets tired. You know about that." Rott shrugged and led Gun into the kitchen. "All maple, see? Old stuff, too. Had this guy buy it for me out of a house in Virginia, old plantation." He cleared his throat, frowning, and tossed his head toward the room they'd just left, backing up the conversation. "But I've had a little rest now and I'm ready to go again. Let me tell you about the deal I made. Beer?"

One *more* door and they were standing in the rear porch. It ran the length of the house, screened in, and looking around it struck Gun that this room, more than any of the others he'd seen, was Rott-like. The inside wall was painted a violent shade of yellow and bore shelves holding a huge collection of beer bottles. Every label, color, and shape. And smack in the middle of the porch was a string hammock hanging from the ceiling, and above it a twisting fan.

"You spend some time out here, I bet," said Gun, accepting a beer Rott had taken from the refrigerator against the inside wall. Some brand he'd never seen, orange and blue label with a picture of a porpoise.

"My favorite place."

Gun was looking again at the hammock, which was pushing an old memory button—he could feel it—but nothing was coming to him yet. He nodded toward it. "Nice. A guy could do some serious sleeping."

"Did this room myself. The rest of the house, I can thank this fag decorator that charged about twenty-nine times what his own hide's worth on the queer market. That's how it is down here, though. Weather makes up for it. Hey, let's sit ourselves down and drink these up."

They walked into the back lawn and sat beside a palm-shrouded swimming pool and didn't speak for a minute or two, watching the leaves floating on the pool's surface. Gun's mind was still at work on the hammock, still coming up blank, when a man appeared from inside the garage and walked toward them. He was tall, and his shoulders were so heavily muscled you couldn't tell if he had a neck at all. He walked like a pigeon-toed cat, light on his feet, gliding almost. He carried a mess of netting attached to a rope, and he stopped at the edge of the pool and tossed the netting skillfully over the water and drew it back toward himself, pulling in the floating leaves and debris and leaving the pool clean.

"Louis," said Rott. "This here's Gun Pedersen, former Tiger, future Hall-of-Famer. Aren't you gonna say hi?"

Louis turned his head and nodded quickly, not smiling, then went back to his netting. Rott tapped a finger to his own temple and said, "He works hard, though. I appreciate people that work hard."

"Are you going to tell me about this deal you mentioned?"

Rott finished his beer and walked up to the porch for another. He looked an offer at Gun.

"No, thanks."

"It's pretty simple, actually. Remember Flax Bundy?"

Gun nodded. A mediocre shortstop in the sixties, journeyman coach in the seventies and eighties, now the Brewers' general manager.

"We got along pretty good when he was coaching at Minnesota. Talked strategy all the time. He taught me a lot. Then last fall we run into each other at the Series. I told him I wanted to come back, and figured I had the head for managing. Well, it turns out they're gonna be clearing house on the big club and bringing in guys that can get along with the new skipper Sirkon. Which means the farm teams get all shook up, too. Some moving up and some down and some dumped altogether. He said he'd think real hard about giving me the triple-A club." Rott sat down with his fresh beer, put his feet up on the table and talked on.

"Shit, not a bad place to start, I thought, so I said to him, 'Think about it? Goddamn. A guy's gotta be able to plan ahead.' So he goes, 'All right then, I'll let you decide. Here's how it is. The job's yours if you win everything down there with your old men this winter. Show me what you can do.'"

Rott took a couple long swallows of beer, half the bottle, then smiled, eyes meeting Gun's for a moment before looking off again toward the pool, and Louis. "That's the deal, Gun. I'm showing old Flax what I can do, and I'll be damned if I don't get that job, too. And from there it's up to the top, only a matter of time. Hell, you and I both know about Sirkon. He can't run a team, the guy's too soft. Brains, all right. But he's a pussy, and after the Sixty-six Series everyone knew it, too, how he tried running around Gauge instead of through him. You watch, he won't last a season."

Suddenly Rott took his feet off the table and looked hard at Gun, said, "Hell, though, what matters right now ain't what's happening to me. It's what's happening to you, my friend. I wanted you out here to get you away from old Mo, and talk some sense into your white head."

10

Cold and tired, Gun pulled into the Gates To Home Motel at nine o'clock. The heater didn't work in the Beretta, and with the sun gone and a wind brisk off the dark, choppy Intracoastal, the place didn't feel a whole lot like Florida—more like March in Minnesota. Fifty-five degrees, the radio said, and going down in a hurry. Frost warnings, oranges beware. A guy might just as well have stayed home. At least up north you knew enough to dress for the weather.

He unlocked his room and found the air not much warmer inside. Attached to the wall behind the door he saw a small oil burner, which he cranked to HIGH TEMPERATURE. Then he put water on to boil on the little stove in the kitchenette. Turning, he saw a distorted image of himself in a toaster sitting eye level on a shelf above the refrigerator. He spoke to it. "Moses Gates is my friend, that's what I'm here for," he said. He'd been saying it all the way back from Rott's farm and figured he had himself pretty well convinced again.

It really wasn't a matter for argument, though. He was doing what had to be done. He knew that. But what you knew in your mind was often the very thing your body wanted to show its backside to, and Gun's body was tired and hurting. Which seemed appropriate, this being Florida. Stomach, legs, back, throwing arm—they all had personal, painful, spring-training memories, and now the knuckles of his hands would, too, not to mention the sore spot on his sternum where this morning he'd taken a punch he couldn't remember.

Sitting down at the foot of the single bed he reached his bruised hands toward the vents of the oil burner. No heat was coming. He got up and turned the dial to OFF then HIGH again, but the unit still didn't respond, so he knelt on the rippled, lime green linoleum and searched behind the safety plate for the pilot. Couldn't find it. Ten minutes later, on his back, fingertips burned from paper matches, he gave up. He let his body relax against the cold floor, hands lying palms up next to his ears. Then he got up and phoned Moses.

"I need some heat in here," he said. "What kind of place is this?"

Moses groaned. "You've got matches in the drawer next to the sink, and the pilot's underneath of that tin plate on the bottom."

"I looked. It's not."

"She's there. You gotta reach way up behind all those little tube things on the right," said Moses.

Behind his voice—right behind it—Gun heard a woman's, sharp and nicked, like a well-used knife. She said, "Make him do it himself."

"You're going to have to come over, Moses. Look, I can't find it," said Gun.

He heard the woman swear and Moses tell her to put a cork in her face. "You shithead," said the woman. "Big flabby-cheeked pink little . . ."

"Everything all right?" Gun asked.

"Twice this good and I'd still be depressed as all get-out. Linda's here."

"I know that. What for?"

"What do you think for? Hiding out. And I bet it's a real hot mystery where she's at, too. This is all we need. My hands hurt like hell and my head's in about ten pieces—Hey, leave that be! Just leave it alone."

Moses's voice strayed from the phone, then came back again. "You know what I'm saying, Gun? My whole body suffers. Don't need any more of this."

"What're you gonna do?"

"Sleep and figure it out in the morning. I'll put her in number ten for the night, way down at the east end next to the road. That unit's got a back door on it, and she hears them coming she can sneak out. Hey!" Gun heard something break, a thrown plate or a heavy glass, then he suffered the sharp blast of a fallen receiver. He massaged the inside of his ear with a finger and waited.

"Gun? Hey, sorry, man. The broad's looned out. My favorite lamp, the one my mom had next to her bed? Hey, damn it! Gun, call you back."

Holding the receiver a safe distance from his head, Gun said, "Fine."

Fifteen minutes later he heard Moses and Linda walk past his door toward number ten, yelling in whispers like people do only if they've known each other in a certain way.

Ten more minutes and Moses tapped on Gun's door and stepped inside. He wore an orange ball cap too small for his graying head and a T-shirt that showed the broadened and fallen condition of his once-solid torso. He looked like a man who had every right to despise the law of gravity. His face was wider than it was long and, for a heavy man, well marked by wrinkles. His mouth was small and puckered, careful. He was shaking, from the cold or something else.

"Not used to this kind of weather," he said. He struggled with his fingers, which wouldn't hold still to let him touch the cardboard match to the lighting strip. When he finally had a flame, he sneezed and blew it out.

"Here, get on the floor," Gun said. He directed Moses into position at the base of the oil burner. "Okay." He lit a match and handed it down. In a moment Gun heard the *foosh* of combustion.

Moses got to his feet—he had on socks but no shoes, Gun saw—and stood close to the heat louvers, rubbing his upper arms with the palms of his hands.

"How'd you get rid of her?" Gun asked.

Moses smiled. "I had this brand-new quart of Comfort I was saving up against the next piece of bad news. She saw it and turned to mush. I *let* her see it, pretending like I didn't want her to. Helps when you know a person's religion."

"I belong to this hot chocolate cult," Gun said. "Want to join?"

"Owahhh, that heat feels good. Yeah, count me in."

Gun took two small, robin's-egg-blue cups from the shelf and filled them a quarter full with powder from the can of Swiss Miss he'd stopped to pick up on the way back from Rott's. He filled them with water from the top of the stove and stirred. "Tell me something," he said. "*You* played ball with Weiler. Tell me about his family. What his dad did, where they lived, stuff like that."

Like a fat bird on a vertical spit, Moses was turning himself slowly in front of the heater. He didn't stop rubbing his bare arms. "Oh, Lord, that woman makes me cold," he said. "You don't know . . . I'm starting to feel better now, though." He took a deep breath and released it slowly, his cheeks puffing out. "No, Rott never said a lot about his people. He talked baseball, and women sometimes, and he liked to read quite a bit, history and stuff like that. Considered himself a smart guy, I'd have to say. But personal things? You didn't jaw about that shit with him, it wasn't his way. And if it had been, he probably wouldn't of said anything to me. The boy had a case of the nigger fright."

"He's a bigot?"

"I don't know what you call it. All I can say is, he had this need to leave whenever I came around. Who knows why."

"So you don't know his background. Nothing at all."

"Did *anybody?* You know what he's like, that sneaky way of looking at you, without looking at you. Look, I know what he thinks of me and the kind of chatter he's spreading. Fine. He can have his opinion, and tell the world, too, but a bear don't shit in the buckwheat if I'm gonna let that asshole get to me." Moses took a sip of his cocoa. "Oww, you're a prince, Gun." His hands, wrapped around the mug, were so big it was invisible. He leaned down and breathed in steam.

"One thing I do remember, though. This is funny, too, and everybody knew about it. Rott had this hammock he always brought with him on the road. No matter what kind of a bed they give us, and most of them awful nice, too, like sleeping in feathers and perfume—no matter. Rott had this hammock he strung up. We're in the Hilton or the Ritz, pricey suites with live plants and shit, and Rott strings up his hammock to sleep in, all night. Ties it up to the bedpost, curtain rod, anything. Don't ask me why. I guess he couldn't sleep anywhere else. And it's not even a decent hammock, but this old raggedy thing looks like it's made of twine or something. He just loved it."

"The guy grow up sleeping in those things?"

"Like I said, I don't know anything about him. But I'm a country boy, and growing up, I knew kids slept in hammocks, homemade ones, on account of their parents couldn't find beds for everybody. Didn't know about real beds till they were shaving and planting seeds. But Rott, no. He always had manners, seemed to know how to eat in fancy places. Wasn't like he came in from the hog house. Tell me, Gun. Has he got a hammock out there on his little farm?" Moses laughed, showing two rows of gold molars on the bottom deck.

"Back porch," said Gun, "and well used, it looked to me."

"That boy is weird, all I'm gonna say." Moses shook his head and drained his mug. "Now I'm going to bed. I deserve it, don't you think?"

"No more than I do."

"See you tomorrow," said Moses. When he left, the cold wind jumped inside.

Gun went to the phone and dialed information. Michigan area code. "Traverse City," he told the operator. "William Stanton."

11

A better fisherman than ballplayer, Billy Stanton had done fifteen years with farm clubs and never reached the big leagues. Good glove, no stick, is what people said, and they were right. Now he owned a forty-seven-foot boat that could handle Lake Michigan any day of the year, and he ran the best fishing outfit on the eastern shore. The major leagues, finally. And no retirement in sight.

In the early sixties Gun had spent a single season with Billy in the Coast League, triple A. They got to be friends: patrolling the outfield on workdays (Gun in left and Billy in center), ocean fishing on days off, rooming together on the road. Then Gun went up to Detroit, where he did what he'd always planned to do with his life—hit baseballs very hard. He did it for seventeen years and made a point of never losing touch with his old friend.

Lucky for Gun, Billy—who had also roomed a year or two with Rott—was home tonight, and Gun was able to pick his brain. Weiler, Billy said, was Missouri-made, southeast corner, tiny town the name of which Billy couldn't recall, though he'd seen it in writing probably a hundred times on letters Rott got from his mother, a faithful writer.

"Money in the family?" Gun asked.

Billy laughed at this. "Those letters she sent him? They always came in used envelopes. You know, they'd been turned inside out and addressed in pencil. I'd say white trash."

"If that name comes to you, give me a call back," Gun said.

"What's up? You sound serious."

"Nothing, probably."

"I'll do what I can."

Half an hour later—it was past midnight and Gun had fallen asleep—Billy phoned with the name. Harristown, Missouri, population six hundred fifty-eight, according to the atlas he'd looked in. Gun wrote this down, thanked Billy, and went back to bed.

The scratching came from way off in the distance at first, then it was much closer, and finally right up against the edge of Gun's sleep. He woke with no idea where he was but sure that someone was at the window next to his head. He opened his eyes and saw a silhouette behind the curtain, crouching. Whoever it was was working something sharp up and down against the louvered plexiglass. Gun lifted the curtain and saw a woman outside, smiling at him. She held up a knife no bigger than a bottle opener, its blade narrow and twinkling in the light from the yard lamp.

"Been here five minutes," she said. "You sleep hard."

Gun just stared. He saw she had rotten teeth and

full lips. A lot of hair, and a lot of nose, and a lot of eye.

"You inviting me in or letting me freeze my jeans off, or what?" she said. "Come on, slugger, find your manners." She stood up and moved toward the door. Gun sat up and thought, First get out of bed and put your pants on, and by then you'll know what's going on. He followed his own instructions, and sure enough it worked.

He opened the door and said, "What do you want, Linda?"

She pushed past him into the room. He looked for the knife but didn't see it. In her hands was the bottle of whiskey.

"It's warm in here, thank goodness. My room's cold as hell on Sunday. Hey, you're safe. Loosen up, smile, you're in Florida."

"I just figured that out," said Gun, glancing at the clock. It was five-thirty.

"And my friends call me Treasure. Moses, too, but not anymore. Now he'd like to be rid of me, so it's Linda." Her face had a ninety-proof glow that more than did justice to the smell of her breath. Gun angled across the floor toward the phone.

"Don't call him, slugger, please. Let him sleep. What I got is for you, anyway. I gotta tell you something confidential. Moses finds out and I'm hamburger."

Gun pulled a chair out from the desk and offered it to her. She sat down and quickly stood again. "What is it?" Gun asked.

"That light just kills me, you know?" She was squinting up at the fluorescent ceiling fixture Gun had snapped on, protecting her eyes with a hand. He reached over and killed the switch.

"God, thank you." She moved over and sat down on the rumpled bed, nestled the whiskey bottle be-

tween her thighs. "I'm so glad you were up," she said.
"I've been thinking all night how I had to see you, and
grew about fourteen ulcers." She rubbed a hand on
her flat belly, lifting the gray T-shirt that covered it.
Her black leather biker's jacket was unzipped, and the
T-shirt was cut low to show her wide loose cleavage.
She leaned forward and attached her huge brown
bloodshot eyes to Gun's. "You know why they call me
Treasure?" she asked.

"No idea, sorry," Gun said, thinking, It's probably
not your teeth, your charm, or your taste in clothes.
Moses, Moses.

"It's when I was little and liked to hide things in the
sandbox, and once Antie Bernice who raised me like
her daughter had this pearl necklace she got from her
fiancé that ran off and got killed, and I buried it in the
sandbox out back of her trailer. Actually it wasn't a
sandbox, it was a sand pit her daddy owned, no good
anymore, all used up and half full of water. So I buried
that necklace of hers and couldn't find it again."

Linda got up from Gun's bed and walked to the
cupboard above the sink. "You got anything to drink
with?" she asked. "I can't stand the feel of this thing
on my lips." She traced a finger around the glass
mouth of the bottle. "Makes me feel cheap and awful,
you know?" She opened the cupboard and took down
a high clear glass stenciled with pheasants in flight.
She half filled it and returned to the bed. He didn't
move from where he sat at the small table. Linda
frowned at the glass for a while then took a swallow.

Gun said, "You were going to tell me something."

"How I got my name."

"No, before. You said Moses shouldn't know about
it."

"I'm working up to that, damn it. Can't you tell?"
Her voice was sharp all of a sudden, her wet eyes dark
and crazy. "A woman that's worth anything doesn't
just lay it all out there, does she? No, she sets a nice

table, everything just so. That's what my Aunt Bernice always says. And then when it's time, and she's ready, she says so. But it's up to her." Linda took another swallow of the whiskey and Gun watched her eyes roll up into her head. They came back even brighter than before.

"Finally I told Antie Bernice that I lost her pearls in the sand and wasn't sure where. After that, we started this game called Treasure Hunt after supper every night where we'd go outside and dig with a couple of cooking spoons and pretend we're hunting for pirate treasure on this island full of fruit trees and naked people. We found the pearls after a couple days that way but then I kept hiding them again because of how much fun the game was. And pretty soon I'm the Treasure Girl to Antie Bernice, and then just Treasure.

"Antie's the only person that ever believed in me. She's the one that said I'm worth something and shouldn't just give it away like milk at the dairy show. She said, 'Treasure, you wanna watch yourself. Men don't go payin' for the cow if they can get the milk for free.' And I'll tell you, Mr. Slugger, I *do* watch myself. Nobody gets to me just like that, oh, no. You wanta see something?"

Gun said he wasn't sure. Probably not.

"Show you anyway." She took another gulp from the glass, then stood up and unzipped her jeans. Gun sat, a prisoner of surprise. Her panties were white, and with the fingers of both hands Linda pushed them down just enough so that Gun could see a fine-link gold chain that encircled her hips. With a single finger she reached down farther and flipped out a tiny leather sheath that held the little knife Gun had seen earlier.

"Antie gave it to me, to protect myself. 'Put it someplace safe,' she said, 'and use it only if you have to.' And I've had to. Cut those sniveling weasels." She smiled, opening her lips to show the blackened tips of her teeth. Then she plucked the knife from the sheath and held it out in front of her on one palm. "Not now, though. I trust you, slugger. I don't need this with you." She set the knife on the table in front of Gun, who decided it was time to leave.

He stood up and reached for his sweatshirt hanging on a hook by the door.

"Where you going?"

"Out."

"Then you'll miss what I got for you."

"That's the idea." He swung open the door and Linda clapped her hands loudly one time, stopping him.

"Moses wasn't with me the night before last," she announced. "We both lied to the cops."

"Say that again?"

"Come back in, I'll tell you."

"I can hear just fine from here."

"Okay, slugger." Pouting, she replaced the knife, tucked the sheath back into her panties, and daintily zipped her jeans. "How's that? Feel safe now?" She picked up her glass from the table and polished it off, then shook her head like someone fighting a sneeze and said, "Phoo, that's awful, pour me another." She collapsed onto a chair and let her arms fall straight to her sides, her knees splay out. Her lips moved soundlessly as Gun poured out a couple swallows from the nearly empty fifth.

Linda's nose wiggled and sniffed and life returned to her limbs and she gathered the glass in both hands, held it close against her chest. "What were we talking about?" she asked.

"You and Moses. The night of the murder. You said you weren't with him."

"Oh, yeah," she said, and took the smallest taste of whiskey.

"Let's hear it."

"Everything I told them, it was all made up. The other night? That's the first time he called me in months, and said, 'Treasure baby, do I need you right now or what?' This is late, too, and I went right over and he tells me about that reporter guy that's a friend of his and what happened to him and his eyes are jiggling he's so scared. And of course I said I'd help. I never turn a body down that's in need, if I can help it." A small grin stiffened her lips. "Of course, I figured maybe he'd be a little more grateful. I mean, I covered his rear and it doesn't seem to make any difference to him. He got what he needed and said so long, is how it went. He's a pig, and listen, I bet he put the rope to that guy after all. That's what I'm gonna tell those detective smarties in the morning. How I never saw Moses till the next morning when he came begging, and how I helped him, being an old friend and all. And then, slugger, his ass'll be in a major sling."

Linda finished the glass of whiskey and shuddered. Her eyes went back into her head again, and she leaned back in the chair. "A major goddamn sling," she said.

Gun reached out and tapped her cheek with his hand until she came back. "Linda? Tell me, where does your aunt Bernice live now? Still alive, isn't she?"

"You think that'd be a hateful thing to do?" she asked. "Sic the cops on Mo?" Her voice was singsongy and she'd started rocking back and forth on her chair.

"It might be, considering you don't really think he did it. Or do you?"

"Out in Phoenix. Arizona. She's got this trailer in a trailer park, very nice. I ain't seen her in years, not since I was a beautician out there in . . . I don't remember the town, Shitsville." She laughed. "I don't know whether he did it or not, Moses. I don't care."

"You want to go see her?" Gun asked.

Linda shook her head and rocked harder. "Bus out

there'd be at least a hundred and fifty, two hundred bucks. I looked into it last year one time."

"And a two-day ride," Gun added. "Tell you what, though, Treasure. I'll put you on a jet plane and have you out there by this afternoon, if you want. You can have dinner with Antie Bernice tonight."

"What's this bullshit? You're trying to get rid of me."

"You got it. I'll put you on a plane and stake you to a good-time fund besides. Turn it down, if you want. But don't think too long, I might change my mind." Gun stood up and took his car keys from his pocket and jangled them in front of her. "You coming or not?"

"Stake me how much?" asked Linda. She looked surprisingly alert all of a sudden.

"A grand, how about? No more."

"I take it we're ready to leave, then."

By the time they reached the West Palm airport the light was already hitting the high interstate east of the runways. Gun bought her a ticket for a ten o'clock flight, one-way, then stopped at American Express for the cash. Linda disappeared into the women's room and came out half an hour later looking about as good as a woman could who's been up all night drinking and owns a mouthful of bad teeth.

When he left her at the right gate, she gave him a full sour-tasting mush on the lips, then he drove across the street to a Denny's where he drank five cups of coffee and fell asleep.

12

He didn't make the ballpark until two thirty, after a much-needed nap, a good long shower, and two phone calls to Harristown, Missouri.

The first one he made to the newspaper office. The woman there said she knew of Rott Weiler, the ballplayer, and as far as she could remember, his mother lived outside of town a few miles. She wasn't able to find a phone number, though, and Gun didn't tell her that Rott's mother was supposed to be dead. Next, on a long shot, he called the Harristown Baptist church and talked to a secretary, who said it wasn't her place to give out information, but she'd give his question to the pastor, who was out on calls for the day. Gun thanked her and said he'd be waiting to hear.

The game was entering the seventh inning when Gun arrived, and the scoreboard showed Moses's team trailing twelve to three. Gun spoke kindly to an attendant who recognized him and thus gained entrance to the home team's clubhouse. He found Moses chest deep in a whirlpool bath, watching the game on a television monitor and drinking Gatorade. His back was to Gun, and he jerked around when Gun tapped on a locker to announce himself.

"Hey. Tell a guy you're coming, why don't you."

"How're you feeling?"

"Not good," said Moses. "What do you think? Look

at these guys." He nodded at the monitor. The Patriarchs' shortstop and second baseman, after converging on a high pop fly in short center, both stepped back and let it drop. With two gone and runners going, guys scored from first and third, and the batter ended up on second. Moses groaned. "A week ago that's not gonna happen. I had things screwed down tight as a ship in a blow, and now look at 'em." His hands were shaking on the sides of the metal tub. When he saw Gun's eyes on them, he let them slide underwater.

"You've got other worries," said Gun. "Like your alibi for the other night."

"What? What about her? What'd she say?"

"She told me the two of you weren't together, that you called her up and said you needed help."

"That crazy broad."

"She's the reason you're sitting here soaking, Moses."

"Oh yeah? Well, who are you going to believe, me or her?"

"Doesn't matter so much who *I* believe. Who're the police going to believe?"

Moses took hold of the sides of the tub and hoisted himself up. "What'd I ever do, that's what I'd like to know. Where's she at now? I gotta find her." He stepped out of the whirlpool and his feet slapped the concrete floor and he started drying himself quickly.

Gun sat patiently, rolling a cigarette on his knee.

"You sure act concerned about a friend, all I can say." Moses was pulling on his briefs. "Come on, where's she at?" He swung open his locker door and grabbed a large white bottle of baby powder from the top shelf, doused himself with it.

"Not telling," Gun said.

Moses stood in the white cloud of powder and sneezed half a dozen times. When he could breathe again, he rubbed the stuff all over himself, chest, belly, shoulders, arms, legs. He said, "When there's as much of you as there is of me, you need all the help you can get, finding your way into a pair of pants."

As Moses dressed, Gun wondered what it meant if Linda *was* telling the truth, which he guessed she was. Like they said, honest as a drunk. Maybe it meant nothing more than Moses being scared out of his wits. Gun hoped that was the case. But it wasn't making life any simpler. He'd come down here sure of just one thing: his friend's innocence. Now he couldn't even count on that.

"Let's get out of here," said Moses, toweling his hair.

Gun stayed on his bench, shook his head. "Not till you tell me if Linda lied for you."

"So you believe her over me. Okay." Moses didn't look at Gun as he spoke. There was a lot of pout in his voice.

"I'm not asking anything you wouldn't be asked by someone else," said Gun.

"You're not somebody else, though." Moses's eyes roamed a little, then found Gun's face. "I stuck by you, remember."

Gun hardened his gut to quell the anger there, clenched his fists and consciously relaxed them. "Look," he said. "I'm down here, right? That ought to tell you everything you need to know. Don't give me any of that loyalty crap." From behind, Gun heard the clatter of cleats on cement and he turned to see Rand Bellows and Longie Pratt, Moses's right and left fielders, dragging in from the runway. Their jerseys were open and Pratt was yawning.

Moses said, "Not over yet, is it? We still bat."

The two of them nodded at him and sat down in front of their lockers.

"What the hell are you doing?"

"Same thing you're doing. Getting a jump on tomorrow," said Longie. He tossed his glove into the bottom of the locker.

"Be early tomorrow, then. Extra batting for both of you. Today you'd a been gifted to *throw* the ball out of the infield. Come on, Gun, let's get out of here."

Reluctantly Gun stood up and they left by way of the rear exit and followed the corridor running beneath the seats to a door which gave into the parking lot. The Florida sun was still high, and after the dark of the clubhouse it stunned them. They stopped to let their eyes adjust.

"Well, well, the two blind mice."

13

He wore the same suit today, new tie. One of those silly green ones fashioned to resemble a fish, snout resting on his small gold belt buckle. His small hands rested contentedly on the sides of his wheelchair. "We meet again, Mr. Pedersen. Today, however, I'm not taken by surprise. Which means, of course . . ." He tilted his head back and sighted through the bottoms of his black-rimmed glasses, smiling just barely.

"That you're prepared."

"Precisely."

"He's loony, Gun." Moses stepped forward but was deftly blocked by an expert maneuver of the chair.

"And you, Mr. Gates, are an unfortunate, unfit, unfashionable, has-been athlete. But who among us is without flaw?" He reached beneath his seat and brought up the shiny wooden box and flipped open its lid. Quickly he selected a card and turned it toward Gun for response. "A year to remember?"

"You could say that." It was the 1968 Gun Pedersen.

"Full of treasured moments, I would think."

Gun nodded, then smiled, remembering a movie he'd seen where peoples' souls were occupied by creatures from outer space. The man's eyes made him think of it.

"I'd be honored, and slightly remunerated . . ." He offered up a pen, which Gun accepted. It was a Cross, gold and well balanced. "And your card . . ."

"One thing," said Gun, poised to sign. "I don't do business with people I don't know."

The man smiled back now. "I was christened Jacobson Cleary, Jacobson being a concession my father made to my headstrong mother in the days before hyphens. You may call me Jacobson or Cleary, though I much prefer the latter. I wasn't fond of her, my mother, I mean."

Moses said, "We've gotta run, hey, come on. Linda, remember?"

"Ballplayersballplayers . . . ball?" said Jacobson Cleary, licking his lips. "I imagined you senior leaguers might be more domesticated. Which reminds me, I read an article recently—*Psychology Today*— reporting that professional athletes boast a thirty percent higher testosterone level than an average American male." He pointed at the card in Gun's hand. "Across the jersey, on the bottom there. Thank you. And date it, please."

Gun signed the card and handed it back, with the pen. Jacobson Cleary examined the signature carefully, pressing the bridge of his eyeglasses hard against the top of his nose. Then he looked up, tilted his glasses forward again, and said "Thank you. Now, may I ask? Do you know if Longie Pratt is going to leave the park by this door or the other? I recently acquired an old card of his and need his cooperation." His eyes lit up unreasonably.

"No idea," said Moses, who stepped around the chair and trotted off toward his car. "Other door, if he knows you're here," he called over his shoulder.

"I've gotta go, too," said Gun. "Excuse me."

"In a moment—" Cleary lifted a finger. "But first I'd like a progress report. How are you doing on your, uh, case?" Cleary's smile was off center and small, his eyes playful. "Just curious."

"Afraid I'm not doing as well as I'd like," Gun said. "But tell me this. Why is it I have this feeling I'd be doing a lot better with your help?"

"Now that's easy. No doubt you can sense the wide differential between your IQ and mine."

"Must be it," Gun agreed.

Jacobson Cleary touched the reverse lever and his chair whirred and inched backward. "All in good time, as they say. Now, I don't want to keep you." The old man cocked his head to the right and blinked twice, a dismissal.

Gun thought briefly of pushing a little harder, decided not to. Jacobson Cleary didn't seem at all like a man with something to lose. *If he's really got anything,* Gun thought, *he'll make me wait for it.*

He walked past Cleary's silent chair, half expecting to hear the man's voice again. What he got instead was the sensation of the man's eyes striking the middle of his back. It felt like two spots of cold pressure.

Moses sat in his car, window rolled down, sunglasses on, a cigarette pinched in his lips. His fingers, shaking, explored a bruise on his forehead from yesterday morning's fight. "Just tell me where she's staying, Gun—all I'm asking." Behind the glasses, his eyes were blinking. "Please."

Nodding toward Jacobson Cleary, Gun said,

"Spooky guy. Not crazy or dangerous, I don't think. But he sure acts like he knows something."

"Gun, I don't have anybody else. There's just you right now, and you gotta trust me." Moses sucked hard on his cigarette and held the smoke.

Gun crouched alongside the driver's door and rested his elbows on his knees. "You got a watch on?" he asked.

"Four fifteen."

"Okay, that means Linda's been in Phoenix for about two hours. She would've landed at twelve, their time, two o'clock ours. She and Antie Bernice are probably having coffee, getting caught up on old news."

Moses took off his glasses. His eyes weren't blinking anymore.

"Or watching 'General Hospital.' You'd know better than me," Gun said.

"Coffee? My guess, it's 'All My Children,' with enough beer to last through till 'Wheel of Fortune.'" Moses threw his cigarette down and bounced his head once on the backrest. He smiled. "One-way ticket?"

"That's right. But I could always send her another." Gun stood up and went around the front of the car and folded himself into the passenger bucket of the 280 Z, a nice car in its day but sad next to most of the sports mobiles on the roads down here. "You know that stretch of beach down beneath the seawall east of the coast highway?"

Moses nodded.

"I got this friend back home that used to live on the ocean, misses it quite a bit. I was thinking she might like some shells."

"You were thinking she might like *you* better if you bring her some shells."

"She likes me enough the way it is," said Gun.

"A little more never hurts." Moses started the

engine and jerked forward in first gear. "Damn clutch." To their left, in the shadow of the stadium, Gun saw Jacobson Cleary rolling after Longie Pratt, who walked with purpose, head down.

Guiding the car onto the street, Moses shifted from second to third. The engine faltered then revved free from a dead spot and the tires made noise.

14

Later that night Highway 21 West was narrow and dark, not much traffic, and Gun was surprised at how undeveloped the country was out this way. No roadside businesses, no towns, not even many billboards. Just an occasional cluster of squat homes, garage-size dwellings with dirt yards out front and television lights flickering behind curtainless windows, dogs and trikes and broken-down swingsets scattered about. Who lived in these tiny settlements? Gun wondered. How did they live? The land itself didn't seem to offer much. Although the skies were overcast, you could see there weren't many trees, and much of the country was low and swampy. The only signs of agriculture were an occasional fencerow and every few miles, the sharp scent of oranges from groves that must lie somewhere to the south, upwind.

Gun drove fast, windows reeled down. The air was cool—not cold like the night before, but cool enough to help him stay awake, and he needed the help. His tiredness rested above his brain like a stone weight, threatening to drop each time he closed his eyes. Not that he didn't have plenty to keep his mind occupied. This evening Moses had confessed to him that Linda was telling the truth; he hadn't been with her that night. He'd been at home sleeping, he claimed, but there was no one who could verify it. He hadn't checked anyone into, or out of, the motel, hadn't seen or talked to a soul from late afternoon until Billy Apple called him.

"Linda just popped into my brain," Moses had said. "I mean, what would you do, Gun? You find this guy, a friend of yours, hanging in his fireplace dead, and you're thinking, Lord God, this isn't possible, and you're sick to death and then it hits you. They're gonna say *you* did it."

"I don't know what I'd do," Gun said.

"You believe me, don't you?"

Gun wasn't sure what he believed, but he did know what he wanted to believe and for now that had to be good enough. That's why tonight he was driving west toward a place called Indiantown. He'd just learned from Moses that Billy Apple had spent some time there and had spoken the name in passing once in a while. What Moses figured was that Billy must have had a girl out there. "Drive through it sometime and then try thinking of any other reason Billy would hang around a place like that," he'd said.

Now Gun saw what he meant. There wasn't much here. A pair of gas stations, one with a general store attached (the sign read BURT'S SMILE AND TROT), three bars with parking lots full of battered pickups, and out west of town a retirement community, INDIANTOWN RE-TIREMENT ACRES, according to the big sign on the highway. Gun turned in and made a swing through it. Saw nothing but double-wides—acres of them, true to billing—set down in geometric patterns that approximated the layout of city blocks. Nicely cut lawns, though small. Picket fences. Buicks and Oldsmobiles parked beneath carports. An occasional RV on the street. Some very nice flower beds. Modest middle-class lives.

Gun left the trailer park and drove back into town and pulled into Burt's. Inside he bought a bottle of soda from a large cooler full of ice and, paying for it, asked the woman at the counter if she'd ever heard of a guy named Billy Apple.

"He *from* here?" she asked.

"West Palm Beach." Gun took a photo of Billy from his wallet and showed it to her. She ran a tongue across the surface of her bright teeth, turned and shouted into the back of the store.

"Bobby! We got a cop in here."

"I'm not a cop," said Gun.

The woman stared up at him as if trying to read his face. Her complexion was the color of white soap, and she dragged her fingertips down across one cheek, leaving pink tracks. Finally she said, "You're actin' like one. Who's he supposed to be?" She nodded at the picture.

"Friend of a friend. He spent a lot of time around here. You should have seen him." Gun looked beyond her at the man entering through a door that apparently led to living quarters. He left the door ajar, and the blue flickering of a television played against it. Gun heard a child laugh.

"Says he ain't a cop," said the woman.

"That's right, he ain't. He's a ball player, or used to be." The man took the photograph from Gun's hand and brought it close to his face. He was slight and dark and wore a sleeveless jersey that said Dallas Cowgirls. Instead of a drawstring around the top of his gray sweatpants, he'd cinched a narrow, beaded belt, the kind you could find in a dime store for a few bucks. He hadn't shaved for a few days and his eyes, as he looked up at Gun, were brown and crisp, intelligent. "Yeah, I seen him before, a few times. Came in to buy bread, beer, staples. He likes to talk boats, always buys this here little booklet." He snapped his finger on the stack of *Boat Trader* magazines next to the cash register. "He told me he was buying that there ship of Donald Trump's, what's the name?"

"The *Trump Princess,*" Gun offered.

"That one. Real bullshitter."

"Does he have a place here? Any friends you know of? A business?"

"Always alone, pays in cash. Never asks for credit." The man shrugged. From the back, a child's voice called out: "Dad, you're missing the best part. Hurry up." Then the television flashed and the music jumped and the child screamed with laughter.

"Anything else you can tell me?"

The woman shook her head and put her hand against her chest. "Wasn't in here that much, Enos. You know that."

The man shook a cigarette from a pack he took from the waist of his pants, then looked up at the ceiling, his face compressing with sudden concentration. "I might remember more if you gave me a good reason to," Enos said.

"All right." Gun reached for his wallet.

"No." The man's black eyebrows shot together like a pair of magnets above the bridge of his nose. "I said a *reason.*"

Gun found himself looking at his own hand and wishing he weren't so tall, or the other guy so short.

"I'm an honorable man, Mr. Pedersen. I don't want nothing from you. Just to know why you're here."

"I'm sorry." Gun returned the photograph to his breast pocket and looked from Enos to the woman, then around the store, which was empty except for the three of them. "You didn't see the papers, I guess," he said. "The man we're talking about is dead. He was murdered. Someone hanged him."

"Oh." Enos closed his eyes and his lips moved without making any sound for a few seconds. "That shouldn't have happened to him," he said. "Should it? That's no good."

"That's shitty," said the woman. "It's a shitty place. God help him."

"Dad!" the kid called out from the back room. "You coming?"

"And you think you can find the one that did it? I don't think so. That's not how it works," said Enos. The features of his face seemed to harden and his eyes left Gun's and went to the cash register, which he rung open, slammed shut, and opened again.

"What do you mean?"

"Nothing. I don't mean nothing."

"Danny wants you to watch that video show with him," said the woman, moving out from behind the counter. She walked down the aisle between the cookies and soda, adjusting the arrangement of her shelves.

"You said you needed a reason, and I gave it to you. What's the matter?"

"The matter? The matter is he got killed," said Enos. "That's plenty. I'm going back to watch TV with my boy Danny."

"Just tell me what Billy was doing here, that's all. Please do that."

Enos hesitated, one hand on the stack of *Boat Trader* magazines, his eyes on the flickering rear door. "Did you see a billboard coming into town that's got a big white yacht on it? Spotlights aimed at it from the ground?"

"Don't remember it," said Gun.

"Just past the little church over there on the east side." Enos lifted his hands and made an appeal with his eyes that said, That's all you get. Then he turned and walked back toward the door. "Coming, Danny."

Gun drove east to the outskirts of town until he came to the billboard where he did a quick turnaround. The sign advertised MAXIE'S MARINA, LEFT ON IRVING AND HALF A MILE SOUTH ON THE INLAND CANAL. WE GIVE YOU THE WORLD. He followed the directions and parked in the asphalt lot next to a white Lincoln Continental, late seventies model. The marina was small, a single U-shaped dock about the size of a baseball diamond. Most of the slips were filled, but only one boat still had its lights on. Gun checked his watch. It was just past eleven.

The boat was about thirty feet long, with varnished teak rails and a white curving hull that formed a right angle with its own reflection in the dark water. Gun stepped aboard and called softly toward the galley.

"Anybody home?" He stepped down and knocked on the small door.

"Yes, come in." A woman's voice, sharp.

"Excuse me." Gun pushed open the door and bent to show his face. He smiled, trying to look smaller than he was. Not easy here. He couldn't see her at first.

"What do you want?" she asked, and he looked toward the voice. She was back in the corner, her bare feet up on a small table, and Gun's eyes told him here was a woman worth a much longer look than he could politely give in this situation.

"I'm looking for Billy Apple's boat."

"This is it. Billy's dead." The borders of her face were all angles, but there was softness within. She had auburn hair in a braid that fell down in front of one shoulder, and her eyes, Gun saw in the muttering light of a Coleman lantern, were someplace else. On the lift-up galley table in front of her was a six-inch stack of *By-Line* clippings. Billy's columns. She crossed her arms on her chest as he stooped under the low ceiling and did not invite him to sit. In the dim mahogany cabin and enclosing incense of kerosene he felt he had intruded upon worship.

Then her dark eyes placed him and settled into understanding. "Gun Pedersen." A faint smile. "You're looking for my brother. If you're Billy's latest crusade, then you're almost as unlucky as he was."

"I'm sorry. I know about Billy."

"And knowing about him, here you are on his boat. I've got to tell you, that makes you look real good, slugger." She said it calm and bitter as a poisoned lake and Gun thought, Sweet Heaven she's quick. And she was lovely, too. The things you noticed at the wrong times: pretty fisherman's sweater showing such prettiness beneath, no makeup on her and none needed, all this mahogany glow from the lantern.

He said, "I'd like to sit down," and she stretched a stockinged toe beneath the table and shoved out a canvas camp stool and he sat.

"If I'd known you were here—" he began.

"You'd have stayed off the boat. How courteous. What *do* you want?"

He found now that he didn't want to tell her. Linda drifted into his head with her sour breath and tight pants and her pathetic lie for Moses. Moses's own lie, even to Gun, that he'd been with her that night. The deceit boiled in his stomach. He wanted to step out of it all, say good-bye right now and fly north to his lake.

He told her anyway: about Moses Gates, who was no one to her except the man who found her brother, about Billy's interest in Moses, and how there were people now saying Moses killed him, though it wasn't true.

"Why *couldn't* it be true?" Diane said vengefully. "Because he's your great buddy?"

That landed in the solar plexus and took a while to absorb. "Moses was your brother's friend," he said finally. It came out lame and to crutch it up he added, "He was with somebody when it happened." Thinking as he said it, *All this for a friend who lies.*

She believed him though, or perhaps not, but released him for the moment and picked up the top inch of newspaper clippings.

"You ever read my brother's stuff?"

"No."

"For a writer he was damned shy about it. I wanted to subscribe to his paper but he wouldn't have it, told me he'd be self-conscious. Every couple of months I'd get one of those brown envelopes from him with clippings, the ones he wanted me to read." A smile surfaced briefly and Diane pushed it under. "I'm older by three years but he was protective. Always. All those years he's down here writing away and I'm up in Boston thinking he's Charles Kuralt, doing sweet stories about ninety-year-old canoe racers and old guys getting through spring training just one more year."

"You didn't know about the other stories."

She snorted, waving clippings. "I heard, once or twice. On the big ones, people I knew saying, 'Hey, that brother of yours, Carl Bernstein.' So I'd call up and say, 'Congratulations—why didn't you tell me?' And always it was, 'Geez, Diamond, I just lucked into it.' I didn't know he was on a steady diet of that stuff. My God, soccer players eating dope."

She quit talking and sifted through newsprint. The Coleman lantern murmured quietly and dimmed suddenly like a bulb on a stormy night, then flared back. She held up a clipping, three columns of print surrounding a photo.

"I remember him sending me this one," she said. "A couple of years ago. It's about this girl and she's from some kind of home for wayward kids. She gets regular grades at school, no dummy but no standout, she's a girl who never got noticed by her parents or anybody else. And then it turns out she can run. Marathons. It's a total shock because one day she just decides to be a runner and in a year she's beating everybody and she's the pride of the school. The track coach is salivating." The smile surfaced again, looked around warily, stayed. Gun reached for the clipping and saw the picture of the girl standing hopeful and slight in running silks, brown hair chopped at the shoulders and a few strands ghosting across her face.

"Billy loved doing that story. He said she reminded him of me." She looked carefully at Gun. "After our parents divorced, Billy was always trying to make sure I felt appreciated. He really was too wise to be a little brother."

"You were a fortunate big sister."

The lantern flared again, gasping the last kerosene. Diane said, almost reluctantly, "You never did tell me why you came."

"I told you about Moses. That whole story."

"It doesn't explain why you came. What did you think you were going to find here?"

She waited, sitting forward now, the lantern throwing frantic shadows.

Gun said, "Nobody found any of your brother's notes from the story he was doing on Moses. We don't know what he learned, or who knew he'd learned it. When I found out about the boat, I thought I'd look here."

Her smile dove for cover then and she stood up taller than he would've guessed, her braid swinging, and spoke with heat. "You think this Moses Gates story is the reason someone killed him."

"Might be."

"But Moses is your friend, so you come here wanting to absolve him!" Suddenly livid as the darkness came.

"I thought if I could take a look—" but he was

talking to himself, she wasn't hearing any more but was going up the four steps out of the cabin and all he could do was follow.

The bright barbed moon had come up quickly and swung like an omen over the mast. Sky almost bitter clear but a low ground mist bringing chill over the marina. Strange night.

"You have to go," she said to him.

He saw her sadness and the moon on her skin and did not want to.

But she said, "Billy did enough for the lost when he was living," and he had no trouble going after that.

15

If you were an old ballplayer, Moses had told Gun— good or bad, if you'd ever made the big leagues—the folks down at the Dugout treated you right. Walk in, sit, they set down a beer. Sometimes you had to pay.

There were no windows in the place, though, and you also had to listen to old ballplayers.

"You laugh," Eddie Viken was saying, "but I don't get many better offers." He held up a clear brown plastic bottle. "They phoned me up, said they'd give me a free grandfather clock if I bought a three-month supply of vitamins. Okay. I buy the stuff and they say, Mr. Viken, sir, could you use some extra income?"

"Hell yes," said a big grinning Cuban.

Eddie nodded. "So they say, Mr. Viken, we'd like to make you a distributor. All you got to do is have two vitamin parties a month, introduce us to your neighborhood, you keep twenty percent of everything you sell."

"Ah, generous bahstads," said the Cuban. He was Thick Fingers Garza and he'd been a rookie when Gun retired. Up-and-down career, Gun remembered. Especially down.

"And you jumped at it." Rott Weiler had the far end of the table along with Harold Ibbins. *Disappearing Harold,* Gun thought, *this time we'll talk.*

"Damn right," said Eddie Viken. "They sent a guy out to see me. Big, soft, fat, never worked a goddamn day. He had a red suit jacket with real gold buttons. He had a Ferrari."

"Oooh," said Rott.

Thick Fingers showed enormous teeth.

Toby Juling said, "You *take* these vitamins of yours, Eddie?"

"Absolutely."

"They gonna get you back to the bigs, ah?" said Thick Fingers Garza. The table hooted and Gun smiled; Eddie Viken had been up for parts of three seasons, pitching middle relief. Gun had faced him a handful of times. It had always been fun.

"You pricks can laugh, you had big contracts. I didn't make shit playing ball."

Rott said, "Worth every nickel," and there was more hooting, and Eddie shut his mouth at last, fleeing to the silent place of the abused.

"Gun," Toby Juling said, "Moses says you're not here to join up." Toby had almost twenty years of third base behind him in the National League and now did it for Moses's team, the Patriarchs.

"Just visiting."

"I guess you used your money right," Toby said.

"Where I live, you don't need a lot of it."

Toby rubbed his beard. It was trimmed close, brown going white. "So tell me what you think of us, Gun. A bunch of old men, back to playing for sandlot crowds, sandlot money. You think we weren't smart enough to quit?"

Earlier that afternoon Gun had stood in the third-base dugout and watched Toby play the corner. The legs were supposed to go before anything else and Gun knew Toby's were going, all that stretching and limping between innings, but when Toby stepped over the chalk he was back in the National League. He felt of the dirt, leaned in, hurt like hell, and made the plays.

It was quiet around the table.

"The way you play it," Gun said, "it's still a pretty game."

The barman arrived and set down another round.

Toby said, "Way I saw you hit old Hector the other day, you're still taking a few swings yourself. You sure you didn't come to suit up?"

"Gun's down here playing Sam Spade." Rott grinned. "On account of the Hangman, here, hey Moze?"

"The hell." Moses protested but he had on a smile. Across the table Gun saw Harold Ibbins's eyes go cold.

"That reporter, ay," said Thick Fingers, a needle of ivory showing behind his lips, "it's too damn ahhh-bvious. You hang one mahn, Moze Gates, you got to find another way the next time."

"Where I walk, bullshit follows," Moses said. He said it in a big voice and in it Gun recognized the *gee-whiz* inflection of the modest aunt who's won the pie contest. And he realized for the first time that in the right company, Moses *liked* being the Hangman. Out in the light, it was scandal and trouble; down here in the Dugout it was attention, and the owner sent you a beer.

"You talk like that, you might be next," Moses was saying to Thick Fingers Garza.

"Man's a killer," Rott said. Next to him Harold was staring dark faced into his glass. He hadn't put in a word since Gun and Moses stepped into the bar and he was leaning slightly away from Rott as if from a backed-up toilet. Harold and Rott had some history, Gun remembered; roommates on the Twins for a while before some clubhouse nastiness happened and set them apart. He'd have to ask Moses about it.

They were coming down to the end of Round Four when the door opened wide and a slight figure in a wheelchair rolled in. The old man moved slowly, craning his neck, checking out tables. The black lacquered box was across his knees.

Toby Juling said, "Tomorrow, gentlemen," and left two inches of beer in his glass.

"You can run, but you can't hide," Moses muttered. "Handicapped, my ass."

"He's after me," cried Eddie Viken. "Must be. He's already got you guys."

The old man had them now and scooted leisurely among tables, taking his time. He arrived finally, swept aside Toby's chair and pulled up. He twisted around in his suit, motioned the bartender. "You. Bring a round. Well, *fellas,*" he said, "how's the game? How're the legs? Still enjoying the *wind sprints,* are we?"

Rott said, "Tell you what, Cleary, I liked this place a lot more before they put in that ramp. Remember those stairs they used to have? Nice narrow steep ones." Rott made a flicking motion with his hands. "I could've helped you down."

"You can go, Weiler. I'm not here to see you."

Eddie Viken had on his first hopeful expression of the day. Weiler stayed.

"Gun Pedersen," said Cleary, "it's always *so* good to see you."

Gun was silent. He saw that the old man wore a

striped tie today and checked the wheelchair. Still
paisley. The bows of his glasses rode high on his
temples. Hunched into the black box, glaring at
baseball cards, he looked like the ripe fruit of insanity,
ready to drop.

"Banks, Henderson, Kaline, Pedersen." The Autograph Man had a handful stacked on the table. "Say,
here's a Rott Weiler. How'd *he* get into this august
company?"

"Take the stairs, prick," said Rott.

"I'll bet you don't remember the day. I do. March
seventh, 1977. Best wishes, Rott Weiler.' Ah, now you
recall." Rott looked to be swallowing a batch of salty
words. Moses had his eyes closed. The old man raised
his voice. "Seven March Seventy-seven, a great day
for our national pastime. Ferdinand Millevich ties a
good strong knot and leaps from the press box at
Tinker Field. This card," Cleary said, studying the
image of Rott, "gratifies my taste for the morbid. Mr.
Millevich considers distances, affixes the knot, and
swan dives, while in a swampy bar across Orlando Mr.
Weiler grins and signs his card for a disgusting old
man in a wheelchair."

Gun saw Harold turn slowly toward Rott. It was the
look of a man who didn't want to be caught looking.

"Here's a fact," said Cleary. "There are better
stories associated with these cards than the ballplayers
themselves would be able to tell you." He held up the
Kaline, Al with the sun in his eyes and the bat
confident upon his shoulder. "This fine Tiger was
attending some asinine high-school sports banquet
when I found him. Little town not an hour's drive
from Chicago. I lived there then. It was the middle of
a very nasty winter and every street had ice. He spoke
about cowardice, wouldn't you know it, damning all
draft dodgers; you ought to have seen the coaches.
How they yawned! But afterward I followed him out

to the car he was renting, a big Mercury, and apprehended him there. He was glad enough to sign, and in fact asked me what I'd thought of his speech."

Cleary stood the Kaline on its head and glanced at Gun.

"Well?"

"I told him it was brilliant. I was younger then. Listen, though: I was leaving the parking lot and a little boy, maybe seven years old, stepped out of the school and saw Kaline. Probably the only kid in the place who didn't get an autograph and he came tearing. Kaline was having trouble with the Mercury, it wasn't starting, and I thought: The kid's got him. He reached the car and got hold of the door handle. Kaline never saw him, too distracted, and at last the car started with a gigantic roar and the little boy's feet slipped on the ice. It was like a magic act, he just dropped, lost the door handle, and disappeared under the car. And then Kaline got it into gear and drove away."

Moses breathed, "Aw, shit," and the old man swiveled on him.

"Thank you for your intelligent commentary. You'll want to know the boy wasn't hurt. I went to him where he lay on the ice, his eyes squeezed shut as you might expect. He'd gone under and simply frozen there on his back, waiting for the car to squash him. I waited. It took him five minutes and not another soul around. He opened his eyes finally, and I told him to go.

"Fifteen years later, in this very city, a thin punk in an alley tried to take that Kaline away from me. He had a gun. Would you like the story of what happened to *him?*"

No one cared to hear it.

"That's all right. No offense taken." Cleary extracted a Thick Fingers Garza, 1982, and handed it over. "Would you be so good?"

Garza signed.

"Thank you." He backed his chair from the table, turned, traveled unhurriedly toward the door and daylight.

Eddie Viken rose and followed.

Outside the Dugout Gun stood squinting with Harold Ibbins against the sudden sunlight. "Well, Harold," he said, "how's the advertising?"

Harold was quiet. Not far down the walk Eddie Viken had caught up with the Autograph Man. The chair was at a standstill.

"Look at that poor jerk," Harold said. "You know what he'd give to be asked for his autograph?"

"You want to tell me about your talk with Billy Apple, Harold? All about Ferdie Millevich, wasn't it?"

Ibbins had his eyes on the sidewalk. "It's a hell of a thing, Gun. You know how you can start remembering something a whole lot more than you want to? Billy Apple, now, he was out at my place not more'n a week ago. I liked him, man, honest to God I did."

"You didn't want your name in the paper."

Harold showed Gun his face. It was tired, the capillaries a little redder, a little closer to the surface. "Tell you what, Gun. I got to go home, sit in the tub, talk to my wife. There's been too much happening."

Down the walk Eddie Viken was doing the talking. They could hear the dull wash of his voice. The old man was looking up at him with his face going dark.

Harold said, "I live down on the water—thirty-two twenty-five Coastal. You come by early tomorrow, Miss Mary will feed you breakfast, we'll have a little history. There may be," his voice soft as flannel, "some necessary doings."

They looked up to see Cleary reach his boundary of patience and cross it without hesitation. He pointed a thin index finger at Eddie Viken and his voice appeared to them with evangelical clarity.

"I don't know you," he said. "Depart from me!" And Eddie quaked and pulled away.

"Lord," said Harold Ibbins. "Lord, Lord."

16

Gun woke the next morning with the smell of bad fish and salt brine curling through the window. A carload of boisterous Okies bent on cod had seized two of the rooms at the Gates To Home and was scraping the innards from each day's catch into Moses's green Dumpster. He went to shower. Behind the plaster wall he could hear someone, not an Okie, crying. Nothing frantic. Just a plain, miserable soak. It seemed at home here. He drowned it with the hiss of warm water—it didn't get hot at the Gates To Home—and put his mind on Harold Ibbins.

The way Moses had it, Harold and Rott had roomed together on the road for a couple of seasons. It worked out, Harold being forgiving enough to live with Rott's hammock *and* his ego. Then one day after a September loss to the Orioles Rott had simply lost his sanity in the clubhouse, grabbed onto Harold and started hitting. No reason, was how Moses remembered it, just plain sudden hatred that hadn't been there before. Rott started rooming with Ferdie Millevich after that.

"And now Rott sits next to Harold in the bar?" Gun had asked.

And Moses had said with a sour smile, "Harold's

rich now, see, living on the water in one of those old-boss mansions. You see what money can buy."

Moses said this last part with the clipped complaining tone some people use when speaking of another's success.

Gun shut off the water and reached for a towel. It was apple-crate stiff. He forgave his friend his jealousies, dressed, and left.

The Coastal mansions were, as Moses said, mostly old money. Oil, railroads, shipping. What Harold had done to merit his own fragile piece of Atlantic frontage was not to play baseball particularly well, but to play it for long enough to teach himself the traps and pathways of the Florida real estate morass. Spring training would come and the Twins would head for Orlando, and while his teammates spent their free hours in pursuit of the pretty magnolias that hung about Tinker Field, Harold would be sitting at the feet of local land merchants. He told everyone it was his fallback career, waiting down south for the day he got cut from the team. Then Florida made one of its exponential leaps in desirability, as if one dark day in January everyone in Michigan and Maine and Minnesota suddenly looked up and saw the same TV ad from the Florida Chamber—"Paradise was never lost, you just haven't been here yet,"—with the woman in that brief bikini and all that beach, not a shadow on it anywhere. Everyone became a believer all at once, the pilgrimage was on, and Harold Ibbins turned to his fallback career. For a utility infielder, lifetime average .227, it was like rolling off a wood cot and landing on a Sealy.

Gun understood something of money but turning south on Coastal he came at once into elegance of disturbing proportions. In the new Atlantic sun the white mansions shone copper and seemed to lean like tombstones away from the ocean. Some of them were so vast he felt he could see the curve of the earth in their rooflines. He met no cars. No one appeared in the big sun-dazzled windows. Lawns stretched away green and sweet with dew, and Gun thought: No one walks on them.

Harold's mansion was only a little less immodest. It was high white stucco with black trim and black shingles that looked like slate, three tall stories with an iron-fenced widow's walk on top and a bed of hibiscus and oleander at the bottom. The flowers went all the way around, contained by a row of some veined jagged stones that poked up unevenly from the earth like emerging bedrock. Gun parked at the curb and didn't lock the Beretta. In this neighborhood, people didn't even *see* Berettas.

He was looking up as one had to do in front of such a place—get this close and it took up so much *sky*—and didn't recognize that something did not belong until he'd pulled his eyes back down to the doorway. He turned left, right. Still no cars, no people, no noise but the sea, no motion but the wind. A salt spray reached and dizzied him. He felt he had seen something but lost it before it got to his brain. He looked back to the mansion and a tiny thing fluttered, high up. His eyes grabbed it and hung on. Up on the peak, on one of the iron spikes that bordered the widow's walk, hung a stocking. The wind caught it and it whipped to the west like a little black flag. A man's stocking. It moved again, and to Gun it looked like the last living thing in old-money Florida.

Harold didn't answer the bell and neither did Miss Mary. A rising ache in Gun's gut told him to get inside the house, and when the door swung open unlocked, it surged up and told him: *too late*. There was a smell inside of blown-out candles. A cheap old-masters print had come off its nail there in the hall and lay cracked at his feet.

"Harold," Gun called.

Nothing, and he was afraid of what he'd find.

The elegant high-ceilinged dining room faced the ocean. It had a dark wood hutch exhibiting old plates painted with Wisconsin wildflowers. Next to it a massive oaken table had been tipped up on its side. On the floor a bone pile of forks, knives.

Through an arch and down a hall Gun found the stairway and slipped going up on something wet trickling down the steps. He rubbed his fingers, sniffed. Water. Chemical smell.

There was more abuse on the second floor. Someone had thrown a rocking chair and put a deep bruise in the wall. At the landing above the steps an enormous aquarium lay angled on the floor, water seeping slowly from a prodigious crack. Goldfish gaped and trembled, going dry.

On the next set of stairs Gun felt in his ears the plain preoccupied hum of happy insects. The house felt suddenly far too warm. He shut his eyes and breathed in through his nose and understood about the bugs. It was not an overpowering smell, not yet, but heavy and still. Ripening. He stopped there on the steps, thought of police and Moses and sickness and every just grounds for turning back. A solitary buzzing broke from the pack and Gun looked up to see a fly, a lone bluebottle, heading downstairs. It was big and a slow flyer, tilting a little from side to side as it went, like a satiated partygoer looking for a place to lie down. Nearing him the fly swerved carelessly at his head and he snapped back in something like panic. His head cracked against the wall, steadied him: *Up you go.*

And then he was up and going room to room and here was Miss Mary at last, in a guest bedroom where all the guests were bluebottle flies. She was on her face, half under the bed. Gun saw four dark pockets

on the white muslin spread and knew they had seen
her hiding underneath and simply shot her through
the bed, and she died trying to climb out. Miss Mary
had hair dyed an unnatural black. It was pulled back
from her face, like they'd checked to make sure it was
all done before they left. The skin on her cheeks was
gray-white and shrunken like stressed leather. Her
eyes were half open, brown. Beneath her, blood had
wicked into sky-blue carpet, and the color was deepest
grape.

Harold was nowhere.

Gun crouched next to the woman and shut his eyes.
His stomach was jumping all over him and it needed
to stop for him to think. There wasn't a reason for
such slaughter, and yet somehow he didn't feel surprised. A fly landed on the side of his nose, another on
his forehead. They wanted to stay and he had to push
them off with his fingers. Damn greedy things, and
hundreds of them. They made a racket beyond belief,
and even here facing Miss Mary he had to wonder
how they'd all got in. And wondering this, he remembered what had seemed so wrong before.

And he knew where to look for Harold.

The steep stairs that led to the roof were behind a
narrow door in what he'd taken to be a closet. He went
up them in the fresh Atlantic sunlight coming from an
open trap at the top. Flies were entering, swooping
down. Twelve steps and his head came out into the
wind. He saw the weather-smooth walk, its iron
handrail. He saw the black sock waving. He pulled
himself to the roof, stepping softly on the slate. The
widow's walk went straight along the peak to a huge
brick chimney and crossed itself in a   , reaching east
and west along high gables. West. At the back edge of
the roof Gun braced, leaned as far as he could over the
handrail, and saw Harold Ibbins lying on his face
among the hibiscus. The arms of his bright sun-
colored robe were stretched forth like wings. His head

had met the jagged bedrock. And even from on high Gun could see the ripped skin of Harold's legs, where he'd tried to snag the iron rail and left only a sock snapping on the salt wind.

17

He was thinking as he drove and waiting for a phone booth to show itself, and finally, just when he thought his luck would hold, he saw one. It sat all by itself on a corner with busted-up curbs, out on the west edge where Palm Beach gives out and turns to flat land and weeds and thin roads heading elsewhere. He dropped in coins, information gave him some, and he dropped in more.

"*By-Line*," said a young man's voice. Preoccupied.

"I'd like to leave a message for Taylor Johns," Gun said.

"She's in. You can talk to her yourself."

"I'll leave the message."

"Whatever."

Gun stooped in the phone booth. He wasn't sure this was the thing to do. Still, someone had to know; and cops could eat your day whole, asking questions. He said, "Tell her to look into an address, Three-two-two-five Coastal. It's the home of Harold and Mary Ibbins. She'll probably want the police to go in first—"

The young man snapped out of his dreamy voice. "Sir, you really should talk to her—"

"Tell her Harold was a source in the story Billy

Apple was doing when he got killed." On the line, a pen scratched paper. "The sweet story," he said, remembering how she'd put it. "The one he *felt.*" He hung up.

Indiantown was more familiar this time around but that didn't make it nice. The main street had a hot afternoon stink. Gun drove straight to the marina, which smelled of good water and clean diesel engines.

Diane was topside on the *Long Napper,* kneeling, soaping the teak. She looked up when he stepped aboard.

"Back so soon," she said, not thrilled about it.

"Feel like a break?"

She stood a little stiffly with her auburn braid falling forward over a plain blue cotton pullover. The sleeves were pushed up over her elbows. Her hands and forearms glowed with oil soap.

"Billy liked this strange Mexican beer. There's some cold." She nodded at the hatch and he went below.

When he came up with two brown bottles she was sitting with the shirt tucked into a pair of drawstring sailor's pants. Her feet—bare and brown toed, not pale Easterner's feet—were propped on the teak handrail.

"You look at home here," Gun said.

"I should. The boat's half mine." She accepted a beer. "All mine now, I guess. Billy was all crazy to have a boat but he didn't have the money. I'd just sold my first script, so I helped him out."

She had a low clear voice that was good to listen to.

"That's what you do? Scripts?"

"When it works out. I tutor part-time in Boston, but it's a flexible job."

"Theater," Gun guessed, stalling. He wanted it to be pleasant, being with her.

"Television, so far. Billy was proud, but he teased

me ruthlessly about it. Contributing to the national anasthetic." She swallowed and put down the bottle and her guard was up again. "I've written enough stories so that I know why you're back. You're the faithful pal. You're still worried sick about this Moses who found my brother because there's bad talk going around, and you're hoping I've stumbled on something that'll prove your buddy innocent."

"Have you?"

She took her feet off the rail and leaned toward him. "Don't you think I want to know who did it? I'll tell you something. I was in West Palm this morning talking to the cops. You want my guess? If it wasn't for the word of some sad woman, I think they'd be crawling all *over* your friend Moses. Because it makes sense. My brother's reopening an old case. What if he digs in the right spot and finds out Moses killed that, that—"

"Ferdie."

"Ferdie—God, you ballplayers and your names— what if Moses *did* kill him? What's he going to do, sit around until the story comes out? Hold out his hands for the cuffs? The only thing on your friend's side is that Treasure woman." She stood up exhausted. "You guys, even your *women* have ungodly names."

Gun let that go by. It was time to tell her. "There's been a new development."

She didn't answer.

"Your brother interviewed someone else for the story. Harold Ibbins, he played for the Twins, like Moses. I went to his place this morning, and he was dead."

She turned to him.

"And his wife, Mary. Dead, too. Harold and Mary. Nice normal names."

She said "Who—" but telling her had made him angry and he cut her off.

"They did it very unkindly, Diane, though I'd

rather not go over it if you don't mind. And no, I don't know who, but I know it wasn't Moses Gates. We were up late last night, talking, and I didn't see him go off and kill anybody."

Her dark skin trembled slightly beneath her eyes. Her fingers went white around the neck of the brown bottle.

"I don't understand it," he said more gently. "But it has to do with Billy's story. It's more than just Moses now—I think anyone connected with that story's in trouble. What Harold told him, I don't know. Not even his editor knows. Billy was too good, no one kept tabs on him."

She sat down again and leaned her head back, closed her eyes.

"You were closer to him than anyone," he said. "Help me put this all together."

"I can't read his mind," she said, and got up and went below and came up with two more bottles of Billy's Mexican beer.

18

"He called me Diamond all the time," she said.

The sun had gotten to where it was doing more than necessary and driven them below deck to shade and a small breeze in and out of the portholes. They had the table up. It was covered with news clippings, wire-bound notebooks, and Mexican empties.

Gun thought the name fit, but didn't say so.

"It was from a game I made up when we were kids,"

she said. "I was about seven, he would have been four. I don't remember the rules except that to win, you had to draw the Queen of Diamonds. We'd play it evenings. He never quit calling me Diamond. Then later he turned it into another game. I'd get home from college, and he would have tucked a Queen of Diamond card into my sock drawer, somewhere I'd be sure to see it, and that meant he'd hidden a present for me."

The notebooks were Billy's, full of names and interviews and story scribbles. Diane had found them in a neat stack in a storage compartment and carried them out in triumph, but nothing came of it. They were full of the wrong stories, the aging athletes, the lonely runners.

"His Kuralt side," Diane said. She said it quietly, leaning close over the pages. "More of the lost."

They went through the notebooks anyway, slowly, Diane's eyes never leaving her brother's quick script. When they were done it was getting dim and cooler in the cabin. She looked up at Gun and he saw the raw grief in her eyes and lips.

"Diamond," she said.

For an instant he forced himself to wonder what Billy Apple had done with the notes for his other stories, the ones that might be worth killing for. Then he saw her again and tilted her face up and kissed her, and stood and went on deck.

It was a while before she followed him. With the day ending she'd put on a white cotton cardigan and sandals. She approached him with the last of the sun hitting her hair and burning it red.

"I'm sorry," she said.

"I should go."

"Not yet." At last there was the trace of something full and sound again in the way she spoke. Her eyes came up and there were laugh lines at the corners. "It was a long day. Stay and eat."

There was almost nothing in the little galley fridge; a loaf of stiff bread, an orange, a few somber Mexicans left.

"I'll get some food," Gun said.

She smiled, opened a drawer in the galley, and lifted out a set of keys on a ring. "Take the Lincoln. Tall man like you."

He stepped off the boat. A new breeze was taking the last of the heat off the marina. She was standing in the cockpit leaning with her back against the wheel.

"Remember the wine," she said.

He thought he could do that.

Cliffert's Greens-N-Goodies was open twenty-four hours for the benefit of Indiantowners venturing out after sunset. Gun parked the Lincoln at the side of the low wood building and went in.

Cliffert's was lit by a few huge racks of fluorescent bulbs that hummed and burned Gun's eyes. The walls were bare and whitewashed but going gray. Hank Williams, Jr., sang from a back room, still surviving. Dust lay in mouse-size heaps upon the shelves. He walked the aisles, squinting. How long did a box of Lucky Charms have to sit to accrue such dust? He stopped finally in front of a crusty aquarium full of green water and lobsters squatting on the bottom.

Okay.

The guy at the counter looked Seminole, with black hair ponytailed and a straw cowboy hat with the sides bent up in a redneck curl. He rang up the lobsters and some spices and cheese and bread and the first bottle of wine Gun had bought in a decade. The Seminole looked at the lobsters with feeling.

"I gotta boy," he said. "I take these little suckers home sometimes, enda my shift. They're good pets, he says."

Coming out of Cliffert's his eyes were so stunned by the darkness that he had to grope for the Lincoln. He opened the door and swung in, holding the bag on his lap.

There was a new smell in the car.

And then a small *hup* of fear and someone who'd been sitting in the passenger seat of the Lincoln shoved the door open and made a run for it.

Only Gun had him by the wrist.

Lord, he wished he could see him.

19

The boy's name was Clarence Coldspring and he had a voice like a bad fan belt, a spooked squeal. He said he'd just been on his way to the marina when he saw Billy Apple's Lincoln sitting in the shadows.

"Who the hell're you, man? This Billy's car, you ain't foolin' nobody."

The dome light showed a slight Indian boy of perhaps seventeen. He had a thin black border of whiskers on his lip, a dozen more curling on his chin, and smooth concave cheeks. His chest looked concave, too. Right for the voice.

"I'm a friend of Billy's," Gun said. "I guess."

The hesitation gave Clarence confidence. He sat up straighter and rolled his head around on his shoulders, loosening up like Canseco.

"We'll be the judge of that. How about if you let go my hand now?"

Gun let go.

"So Billy knows you, man? Maybe we better drive out to the boat right now, you and me. See how *well* he knows you. See if he knows you well enough you're to be handlin' his Lincoln."

Gun thought: Such news I have for you.

"Well, start her up. I got to see Billy anyhow. He needs me, man." The kid rolling his head around.

"Billy's dead, Clarence. Murdered."

The head stopped cold and Clarence twisted in the seat. "Shittin' me, man. Better be."

"Sorry."

Clarence slumped back and said "Aaawww," and Gun saw his left hand steal into the pocket of his jeans toward a long thin lump.

"Leave it there," Gun said.

"What!"

"You don't need it. I didn't kill him." He had a thought and it felt like his first good one in a while. "You think you might know who did?"

Clarence Coldspring eyed him for the first time without apparent cockiness or fear. "You *northern.*"

"Minnesota."

"Friend of Billy's."

"In a way."

When Clarence said, "You damn right I know who killed him," his fan-belt voice was a notch quieter, and Gun nodded and lifted the sack from Cliffert's.

"Back to the boat," he said. "It's lobster."

"Billy was on our side, man," Clarence said. They were sitting in the shadowy cabin of the *Long Napper* while the lobsters danced in the galley pot. "These last months, I was workin' with him. He knew all my family. He came out to the farm. And old Leavitt musta saw him once, and that's how come I know who killed him."

"Wait," said Diane. She had a Bic pen and one of

her brother's old notebooks opened to a blank page. "Back up. We know none of this."

"He was white but he didn't *think* white," Clarence went on. "Listen. Me and my family, we're out on the Leavitt place, a ways east. Fix the machines, make sileage. Used to do the cows. Milk 'em. Round 'em up, move 'em out, raw*hide*, you know? We're about thirty of us now, with the uncles and cousins."

"You live right there?" Gun asked. "On the farm?"

"Two-thousand acres," Clarence said. "There's a little buncha houses the old grandfathers put up, on a back patch. We live there. Wait, though: a couple years ago, old Leavitt's like all the other dairy guys in the world, they're making too much milk. And here comes the government to buy it all up. Leavitt, shit, he don't need no more farmin', so he sells the herd. To the feds, man. Every damn cow. Does this without so much as whispering to a Coldspring what he's thinkin' about. So one day here come the men with the trucks, and we're standin' next to the big barn there. And they start loadin' the cows! I'm just a little kid and I say to my old man, 'Rustlers!' and I'm goin' after my rifle. But the old man, he grabs me and shakes me good. 'Government men,' he says."

Diane said, "My brother knew you all that time ago?"

"Naw. I'm just a little shit at the time. We thought we'd move on, you know? After the cows went. Pick up and find another farm. Only we couldn't. You know how many of these bigshot dairy men sold off?"

"A bunch," said Gun.

"We looked, man. But everywhere was just empty pastures, and the ones that kept their cows, they had workers all over 'em like ticks. Good luck."

"So how'd you stay on with Leavitt, with no work?"

Clarence shrugged, a gesture that made his shoulders fold forward until his chest seemed to collapse. "You just *stay*. We were holed up pretty good, and then one day old Marse Leavitt comes out in his El Dorado. He's smiling like he's half-cocked and he tells the old man, All right, it's hard times. Stay on, do the odd jobs, I'll cut back on the rent until you get some real work."

"And you're still looking," said Diane.

"Us? Hell no," Clarence said. He had that squeal again, it set Gun's teeth at odds. "We haven't looked no more since. You want to hear about Billy, right?"

The kid could tell a story. Gun had almost forgotten.

"There's a couple things happened to us, it's years ago now. First one I guess was old Cleo Coldspring, great-uncle of mine. Cleo would wander sometimes, take a few bottles and maybe a week and come back fulla stink, all sorry. I wasn't even born yet, and one time Cleo leaves and nobody sees him anymore. They kept thinkin' he'd show up. Then maybe ten years ago, I can remember this one, my cousin Loola puts up a tarp, she's gonna camp out, and next morning she's nowhere. Never came back, neither. So. Coupla years ago, pretty soon after the cows went, everybody's sleepin' away in the night, except me cause I got a Big Mac and the special sauce was bad, and I swear I'm hearin' horses. Leavitt's got horses, and somebody's slow ridin', *thunka thunka thunka,* and I'm thinkin' what's the old prick coming for in the night? And then all of a sudden Leavitt, whoever, lets loose with a shotgun. Jump? Man, I was in the *air.* And a big hole opens up in the middle of the front door, he hadda be *close,* and he rides right down the row and four more of our places get it. *Boom boom boom boom.* You wanna soil your jammies, man, that'll do it."

Clarence was grinning, enjoying the telling. Diane hadn't taken a note. She said, "Why would Leavitt do it? He's your landlord, right?"

"Aaahh." Clarence waved a hand in the air. "You think he let us stay to be *nice?* He hates Indians, man.

We're like his hobby. Hey. Some guys got their bass-fishin', some take their dogs, go out after 'coons at night. Leavitt's got Indians, is how I figure."

"Didn't you say anything? Report it?"

Clarence lowered his voice and leaned toward her. "Man, don't you know what lives down here? It's the beast, man, the white beast. It's got big ears. You can whisper, but it hears you." He sat back. "Now here's how I come to know Billy. This shotgun thing has happened more times since—couple times a year, no shit. Always when we're asleep, nobody gets hit but it plows you outa bed in a hurry. Last time was four, five months ago. There had to be half a dozen guys that time, Leavitt's got friends, they musta parked on the highway and come through the bog, 'cause after the shootin' one of our dogs, Early, took out after 'em. Early's got a hell of a nose. Next morning I'm up and looking at the new holes in the siding—it's that cheap fiberboard, man, old tightass—and Early trots up to me. She's all thrilled to be alive because of this new toy she's found, looks like an old rat carcass to me but I take a better look and you know what it is? It's somebody's *braid*. A braid of hair and it's all fulla dirt and junk and there's something on the thick end of it, looks like skin."

Diane's throat made a dry noise and Gun thought: This kid is *used* to bad news.

"I took it to the old man and he starts to cry because it's Cleo's braid, he's sure of it, and we set off with Early. She was sure proud. Took us straight out to the bog and that's where Cleo was, buried shallow in the muck. First time I ever saw my great-uncle and he was a skeleton. And we poked around some more, and you know? Cousin Loola wasn't ten feet from him. So I guess they didn't just wander off and get lost." Clarence stood, rolled his head on his shoulders. "So that's a long one, hey? Mind if I wash it down with somethin'?"

Gun went to the galley. The lobsters were overdone and he turned the heat off. He wasn't hungry. He brought back a Mexican for Clarence Coldspring.

Diane said, "Billy."

"Yeah. We buried old Cleo and Loola right, in nice deep holes, dry ground. Maybe two, three weeks go by, and it does nothin' but rain. Then one day this big ol' Lincoln comes wallowin' in and stops in the muck in front of our place." Clarence shrugged. "It was Billy. First any of us ever saw of him. And he gets outa the car and looks around a little nervous and makes friends with Early. And then he comes in and drinks about three pots of the old man's coffee and asks us a hundred questions about Leavitt. We hit it off, man."

Clarence opened the bottle and took three long swallows that made swishing sounds in the quiet. Gun waited until he lowered the beer and said, "You think Leavitt killed Billy?"

"Leavitt and his friends?" Clarence said, grinning again. "What I know, Billy was on our side. And he was gonna show their asses to the world."

20

Next day, driving back from the grocery store—midmorning and the air heating up fast—Gun sang along with the radio, adding his own chesty bass to the nasally velvet of Randy Travis. The guy made it sound so easy. Gun couln't help feeling a little twist of jealousy. Singer, surgeon, writer, almost anything, he told himself and right now—at this point in life—he'd be peaking. Instead, he was ten years past retirement. You couldn't really blame the poor guys down here in the Senior League for trying to make it all happen again.

In his motel room he unpacked his sack of breakfast makings and lit both burners of the stove, one for eggs and one for pancakes, which weren't part of his routine but it wasn't every morning you found coconut syrup on the grocery shelf. And Krustees pancake mix in Florida? It might just turn out to be a good day. He'd even gotten enough sleep for once.

He drank coffee standing at the stove and did his eggs bright side up spooning grease over the top until the yokes glazed. He mixed the pancake batter heavy on the powder and let them swell up nice and fat on the griddle, eight-inch rounds, and golden. Then he sat down at the small wooden table painted forest green and allowed himself the pleasure of eating slowly. The syrup was remarkably good, sweet with just the right sting and pucker, and it brought Gun a headful of memories. Last time he'd eaten it, his wife was still alive.

They'd flown to Honolulu for their tenth anniversary, and Mazy, seven, had stayed behind with Amanda's mother. For a week they had played in the ocean, gone to bed early, and risen long before the beach crowd for walks along the sand toward Diamond Head. They'd been happy then, unprepared for anything less than happiness, and now, going to that time in his thoughts was difficult but necessary. He felt he owed it to her, owed it the part of himself that demanded full payment for what he had allowed to happen between them. And *to* her. The wrong, of course, was unrightable. Full payment was not something he could provide.

After breakfast, Gun turned to the newspaper he'd picked up at the Winn-Dixie and found the sports

page. The name jumped out right away. Neil Faust.
The columnist for the Minneapolis City Beat had
gone syndicated a few years ago, and here he was. Use
Microscope on Gates, the headline said. Gun read
quickly, not surprised by the strident tone.

If one murder wasn't adequate, maybe four will
do. But I doubt it. Last night Harold
Ibbins—former roommate of Moses Gates—and
his wife, Mary, were found dead at their West
Palm Beach home. Authorities have evidence
aplenty to suggest he was murdered. Police say
Gates is not a suspect. Maybe events of the last
several days suggest that professional athletes in
this country are not bound by the same legal
limits as the rest of us . . .

Gun didn't bother finishing. Faust was the kind of
journalist who'd traded favors for so many years that
he probably sat down at his typewriter with a little box
of IOUs. For reasons Gun didn't know, he'd attached
himself to Moses Gates—those years ago in Minneapolis—like a tick on a heat-stricken dog.

Soon after the death of Ferdie Millevich, Faust had
written several columns painting Gates as the obvious
suspect, a violent man bent on doing Ferdie harm.
Faust's language was pejorative, played to the crowd.
A clubhouse scuffle between Ferdie and Gates, for
example, he'd called, "an unprovoked feral attack" on
Gates's part. Yet the players who were there had told
Gun it was little more than a shoving match.

But there was another reason Gun didn't have time
for Faust's opinions. Several years after the Gates-
Millevich hoopla, Faust was getting his teeth into
Gun's own hide, calling him "a black shadow on our
children's desire for an American hero." He'd also
written that Gun "was as good as a murderer." All
right, Gun accepted both judgments, that wasn't the

issue. But coming from Faust, his own mistakes and tragedy sounded like forgettable soap opera, bad comedy. Pedersen Plays Longball with Starlet While Wife Dies in Pursuit, or something just as bad.

Abruptly, Gun stood and went to the phone. As he spoke to the operator, then placed the credit card call, he tried to remember Faust's voice. Tried to remember it exactly. Smooth, full-throated, vowelly, like a small-time radio personality, is how it came to him.

The phone was ringing now. Twice, three times. Come on, pick it up. Take your fingers off the keyboard and pick up the damn phone.

Five rings. Six. Come on, *I want you on the line.*

"Hello?"

Gun smiled.

"Hello? Who is this?" Yes, just the way he'd remembered, but with a bit more honey.

"Tell me," said Gun. "What do you think Billy Apple learned that Moses might have killed him for?"

"I didn't tell that bastard a thing." Faust's quick answer came as such a surprise all Gun could think to say was, "This is Gun Pedersen." Then the line clicked and Faust was gone.

Gun drove directly to the airport and boarded a noon flight for winter.

21

As the plane began its descent somewhere over southern Wisconsin—probably not far from where
Amanda's flight had gone down—the captain of the
DC-10 came over the intercom with good news. The
temperature at the Minneapolis–St. Paul Internation-
al airport was minus twelve degrees Fahrenheit. The
passengers moaned. Gun wished he'd thought to bring
at least a sweatshirt. He was wearing light cotton
pants, a V-neck T-shirt, and no socks between his feet
and Pony runners.

He hired an airport limousine to drive him into
downtown Minneapolis and drop him at the Eddie
Bauer store in the Foshay Tower, the city's oldest and
humblest skyscraper, dwarfed as it was by the lofty
glass and mirror buildings. Gun had always been of
the mind that a building should look like a building,
and pretty as these new ones were, he couldn't help
but think of them as a kind of architectural lie, ever
vulnerable to the next big windstorm.

The coat he bought was the warmest he could find.
"The most goose down—quality goose down—you'll
ever see in a single garment anywhere," is how the
saleswoman described it. It was red lightweight canvas with a tunnel hood rimmed with coyote fur, and it
came down to Gun's knees. He also bought a black
watch cap, a pair of lined calfskin gloves, wool trousers, a flannel shirt and lace-up half-boots made of

softened bullhide. He paid for it all, then walked into a changing room at the back of the store and put it all on. There wasn't any reason to be cold if you didn't have to be.

Across town, in the lobby of the big gray stone newspaper building, he asked at the information desk where he'd find Neil Faust. The receptionist blinked her large green eyes at the green computer screen and said Neil Faust wasn't in today. Her hair was cropped close to her head and she wore earrings that would put most infant mobiles to shame.

"I talked to him this morning. And I called here to do it," Gun said.

"Well, that's what the message says here." She focused somewhere south of Gun's right ear as she spoke, and he lowered his face in that direction in order to make contact with her eyes. She turned back to her computer. "It says here that he's not in today and doesn't plan on returning."

"What do you mean, doesn't plan on coming back *today?*"

"Yes." She tapped the screen.

"What's his home phone?"

"I don't know—I mean, I'm sorry but I can't give that out."

"Who's his boss here?"

"I don't know." The woman was frowning, pinching the tip of her tongue between her lips.

"What's *your* name? Do you know that?"

Her eyes shot up, caught for a moment, retreated. "Audrey Nelson," she said, and sighed, more tired than angry.

"Audrey, Neil Faust is a sportswriter, right? So tell me, who's the chief sports editor? Give me that person's name, then send me to that person's office. Please, I'm in a hurry."

She shook her head and her earrings made noise.

"Editors cannot accept visitors without appointments. Would you like me to call him and ask if he'll see you?"

"I'd love it. Tell him it's Gun Pedersen."

Audrey punched one digit on her phone and squeezed the receiver between her ear and shoulder. "Mr. Samson? Someone's here insisting he needs to see you. Yes . . . No . . . Gun Pedersen." She nodded quickly. "All right." She hung up and told Gun to take the elevator up to the fifth floor, first door on the right.

"What's Samson's first name?" Gun asked.

"Morley."

"Thank you, Audrey."

The door was a few inches ajar, and a small cardboard sign taped off center to the glass read SAMSON, hand lettered with an ink pen.

"Walk in, if you like." A deep voice from behind the door made this offer, and Gun accepted. Behind a desk that was more than six feet wide sat a man with a potato-shaped nose and a lipless, coin-slot mouth. He was at the deep end of middle age and the hanging fluorescent light above him highlighted the white in his bramble of red hair. He looked dusty—his hair, his tweed coat, his creased face—like if you clapped his shoulder he'd disappear in a gray cloud.

"Sit down, Mr. Pedersen. I've got a kink in my neck, don't make it worse." Morley Samson waved at a leather chair and worked at his upper shoulder with his fingers.

"I don't have time, Morley. And please, call me Gun." He stepped forward and leaned over the oak desk, letting his weight shift to his fists. Morley Samson just looked at him, self-possessed, eyes smiling a little.

"What do you want with Faust? Come barreling in here like this and a guy might take it as threatening. What's the problem?"

"He wrote a column I want to talk about with him."

"About Moses Gates."

"That's the one."

"So what's wrong with tomorrow?"

"Like I said, I'm in a hurry. All I want is the man's home phone, his address. He's writing some strong words about a situation I'm trying to make sense of, and I'd like to know if he can teach me something. People are getting killed down there, and Faust seems to think he knows who's doing it. I want to know what he knows."

"Neil's columns are opinion, you understand. If he knew something concrete he'd go to the people that count. He's been around, he knows what to do." Samson leaned back in his chair and his nose twitched, just a hint of nervous anger, but it was enough to nudge an old memory.

"Where've we met?" Gun asked. He took his fists off the desk and sat down on it, one haunch off, one on.

"I covered the Twins during the sixty-eight season. World Series, too. We spoke a few times. You weren't much of an interview."

"You weren't much of a writer."

"Thanks."

Gun said, "Remember that night, I think it was after game three, and you came into that little seafood place on the south side? It wasn't too late. Kaline and Freehan and I were eating shrimp and watching boxing on TV."

"Yeah, I remember. I was there with Kate Masters. She was writing for *Sports Illustrated.*"

"Right," said Gun.

"Later she met this guy from town here and they got hooked up. Professor type of guy. He runs this bookstore in St. Paul now. Anyway, Kate took a job with us, features. She was burned on sports. In fact, she only left us a year ago. Trying to write novels or something, I guess."

"She's a classy woman," Gun said. "My guess is, she'll do all right. Tell me, what's her last name now?"

"Burning. They call it Burning Books, see." Samson shook his head, entertained.

Gun stood up and told the man good-bye.

"So, coming back tomorrow?" Samson asked.

"I don't think I'll need to. Thanks for the help." Gun walked back toward the door.

"What do you mean?"

"Forget it. Do you want it open or shut?"

He found a pay phone on the first floor and let his fingers walk to the Books section of the St. Paul yellow pages. He dialed the number for "Burning Books, St. Paul's Most Complete Special Service Bookstore." Kate was there and happy to hear from Gun Pedersen twenty-odd years later. They traded updates and scolded themselves for not getting in touch, living as they had in the same state for so long now. When it was comfortable, Gun asked if she knew Faust's phone number or address.

"I know he has a home in Robbinsdale, but I couldn't tell you his number, Gun. Listen, though. If he isn't at work, chances are you'll find him at the Hardbody Fitness up on Highway Thirty-nine. He's over there lifting weights, or pedalling those stationaries every afternoon. Or at least he was last year. Some kind of midlife muscle scare. He looks pretty good, though."

Gun brought the conversation to a polite close and said he'd stop by the bookstore sometime when he was in town. She said he'd better. Then he called for a cab.

22

He felt like a bear among swans. The place was lined with mirrors and alive with sleek bodies in spandex, their owners jogging, swimming, twisting, and stretching their way toward sleeker bodies in spandex. Almost immediately a woman bounced up to him and asked for directions to Alaska, gave a little tug on the coyote fur. Gun said he'd tell her if she showed him how much she could bench press.

"I'm June," she said. "Follow me." She was nice to follow and Gun had to remind himself that places like this made him want to throw up.

They walked—ran, almost—up a flight of stairs, down a corridor overlooking an Olympic-size pool and past a gymnasium where middle-aged men huffed through a basketball drill. Then they were in the weight room and June was on her back at a Universal machine, legs spread, fists wrapped around the rubber grippers of the bench-press bar. She easily pushed it to full extension, let it fall, and repeated the action several times. Sitting up, she said, "One forty-five, I only weigh one ten." She tested the cut of her teeth with her tongue.

"That's impressive, June. *You're* impressive."

"I know. You thinking about joining up?"

"Not especially. Should I be?"

"Take your clothes off and let me have a look to see." Her tongue came out again.

"You qualified to tell?"

"I work here, I'm paid to tell." Her eyes were nice, though, coffee colored, not as well trained as her mouth. "Hey," she said, "have a look around, and then if you decide we've got what you want, come on down to the desk on the main floor and ask for me, and I'll sign you up. And you know what else? I'll initiate you for free, save you three hundred bucks." June was on her feet, moving away, sticking her tongue out at him.

"Free initiation," said Gun. "I'll remember that."

"Remember *me.*" June spun on her toes and loped away.

Gun had already unzipped his red parka, but now he removed it and folded it beneath one arm as he walked toward the cluster of men at the back of the mirror-lined weight room. They worked the free weights, middle-aged white men listening to rap music. Real men, you could tell, serious about their business, wearing gray sweatpants and sleeveless, ripped T-shirts. Everybody else in the whole building had on the shiny body advertisers. All five of the men turned toward Gun as he entered their small domain. None smiled.

"Anybody here know of a guy named Neil Faust?"

"Sure do." The one that answered sat straddling a curling bench, arms resting on a support pad as he worked a loaded barbell. He was improbably bulky in the shoulders and chest and the veins ran like small garden hoses through his forearms. He wore his black hair in a ponytail and the loose skin on his neck told the truth about his age. Pushing fifty, likely. Same as me, Gun thought.

"I'm wondering where to find him. Somebody suggested here."

"What's your name?"

"Pedersen."

"Well, Mr. Pedersen, I'm here to tell you Mr. Faust doesn't want to see you. He seems to think you're a man with a grudge, and he says in his business there're way too many grudges coming his way. So you can just give me a message, all right? And then leave." He cocked his head toward his friends, who smiled to themselves as they strained against their steel.

"You know where he is?" Gun asked.

"Course I do." The man stood now, straddling the bench. He was quite a bit shorter than Gun, probably six feet, but wider by a long margin. Went about two-sixty. "And you know what? I don't mean to tell you." He reached out with a toe of his sneaker and nudged up the volume dial of the boom-box sitting on the floor, then rocked his head a little to the rap beat and lifted his eyebrows. "Well?" he said.

Gun didn't say a word or move. He could tell he didn't have to with this guy.

"If you're gonna just stand there, you might as well be doing something." The man hoisted the curling bar to his chest, went to a palms-down grip with a snap of the wrists and let fly with a grunt. The momentum and weight carried Gun backward but he found his balance, juggling the bar to a comfortable place in his hands, then stepped forward and made as if to replace the thing in the Y-shaped supports of the bench. Instead, at the last instant he snapped the bar to his chest and thrust it straight into the weight lifter's unprepared gut. The man made a sound that no culture in the world could mistake for language and he sat down hard on the bench, the barbell coming to rest on his thighs. He pawed at his midsection, his face stuck in a pain-grin. Gun bent down and yanked up one end of the bench, tipping it and the man backward onto the padded floor. The guy sprawled belly up, inertia sending the chrome-plated bar climbing up his chest, one cluster of circular weights resting on the floor to his left, the other bobbing in the air to his right.

Gun kicked the bench out of his way and checked on the man's friends, who watched but showed no signs of interfering. He knelt at the man's head and looked at him upside down. He repositioned the bar so it pinned him down by the neck. "Don't keep me any longer," he said.

The man couldn't find his voice, but he still didn't look cooperative. There was a lot of mad in his eyes.

"So far all you've seen is defense, pal, and I don't think you're up for the other side of my game," said Gun.

The man sucked air, coughed, and sucked again. He shook his head and reached for his throat, apparently checking the condition of his breathing and talking apparatus. He blinked water from his eyes.

"Where is Faust?" Gun said. Feeling eyes, he looked up and saw a crowd gathering at the other end of the weight room where it gave into the corridor.

"Jack Knife Lake." The man's voice was rough and splintery. He coughed again.

"He got a cabin there?"

"Yeah, but I think it's the fish house where he's at."

"You think?"

"The fish house, yes." The guy tried to push the bar away from his neck but Gun didn't let him. "He drove up this afternoon, early. Said he'd be there a while. You'd be coming."

"Which end of the lake. Upper or lower?"

"No idea, really. I don't know. I told you everything, all right? Now let me the hell up." He coughed again, so hard his thighs lifted off the floor. Gun freed him from the bar, then looked at the other lifters, who were going about their business of getting strong like office workers being observed by the boss.

Gun picked up his red parka and walked out

through the gathered crowd of taut flesh. One pair of eyes caught his attention, dark and wrinkled with excitement.

"Hey."

He nodded and moved past her.

"You come back, *any*time," June said.

23

There was a Perkins across the street, and Gun used the pay phone located in its frigid entry, right next to the door. People were coming and going—it was the dinner hour—and the cold wind stiffened his fingers as he dug the credit card from his wallet and placed the call to Stony. Jack Be Nimble's Bar and Grill. No answer. He blew into his hands and tried the Stony *Journal*.

Carol picked up the phone in the middle of the first ring, her voice all journalist. Then she heard who it was and the edge fell away. Gun's insides warmed, then tingled with shame, remembering Diane Apple and the moves she made without even trying. Even wrapped up tight in grief.

"Yeah, Minneapolis," he said.

"So you're coming up. Oh, God, that's the best news. It's been so cold."

"I'm not coming up, Carol, not now. I'm here to see Neil Faust."

"Ah." He could hear both the disappointment and her unwillingness to let him hear it. They weren't to the stage where you liked to admit any need. "I read that column of his. I thought you might be interested."

"Apparently that's what he thought, too, and he's made himself scarce. Carol, I need to get in touch with Jack. I just tried calling his place and he's not there, but I think I know where he is."

"If Jack's not around, maybe *I* can help you."

"Carol, you know I'd call you in a minute. But this time . . . I've got to talk to Jack."

"So tell me where to look." She spoke a little too fast.

"Mary Magdelene's."

"There a funeral?" Carol asked.

"No, it's—"

"Do you realize what time it is, Gun? It's six o'clock."

"Yup, and Jack should be at his place, drawing a beer for somebody or frying a burger, but he's not. This happens every couple months. He kicks everybody off their stools and out the door and hangs a sign up that says back in an hour. Then he's off to see Father Barnstead."

"For what?"

"Confession, I guess you'd call it."

"That's nuts. Why doesn't he go in the mornings, before he opens his place?"

"You'd have to ask him. Look, could you run over there for me? And then have him call me? I'll be at . . . let's see." Gun relocated the phone number of the car rental agency he'd found in the yellow pages, the one closest to where he now stood. He gave Carol the number. "Tell him I'll be there until seven. If he doesn't get back to me before that, I won't be around."

"And then what?"

"He can forget it."

"And there's nothing I can do."

"Not right now. I'll call if that changes, I promise."
He kept his voice as far away from her as he could,
speaking slightly away from the mouthpiece.

"Take care of yourself, Gun."

"I miss you, Carol." He waited for a response that
didn't come. Then hung up without saying more.

Another cab trip and Gun was at Hertz, Northside,
where he rented a black Ford Taurus, then waited with
a giant-size coffee strong enough to make up for his
sleep deficit—or make him feel that way for now.

He was pretty sure Jack would call. Carol would
find his rusty Scout parked out front of Mary
Magdelene's wide granite steps, and soon Jack would
appear, face broad with contentment, wide shoulders
squared to the world. He was a man of simple notions
who didn't spend a lot of time questioning the impon-
derables, one of the rare people Gun had met who still
knew what he believed and lived by a set of rules. In
Jack's case, you told the truth, you helped your
friends, and you didn't swear in mixed company, and
if somebody else did, you set him straight in one hell
of a hurry. You did all these things the best you could
and then, because you were human and full of shit,
you went to the priest when it got piled up too high
inside. Get rid of it, start over. There was nobody in
the world Gun trusted or respected more than Jack
LaSalle.

At ten to seven the phone rang behind the rental
counter and the man who answered said, "It's for you,
Mr. Pedersen." Gun stood and drained the last of the
coffee, mostly grounds which caught in his teeth.

"Jack?"

"No, Mother Teresa. What's your problem this
time?"

"I'm trying to remember. You've trapped a few
weasels in your day, haven't you?"

"Anything you need to know about weasels, ask me.
Weasel expert. Runs in the blood, French trappers,

right? I can find 'em, catch 'em, and skin 'em. I can *think* like a weasel. Why do you ask?"

"I'm looking for a weasel by the name of Neil Faust, and it's hiding out someplace on Jack Knife Lake, probably in a fish house."

"You've got a thousand fish houses on that lake, Gun. Minimum. Which end's he on, upper or lower?"

"I don't know that. Why do you think I called you? Here's the thing, I thought maybe you could take one end and I could take the other." Jack Knife Lake was fifteen miles long and made up of two separate bodies of water, connected in the middle by a narrow channel. Gun had fished it many times in the winter and knew there'd be two main icehouse settlements. One extending off a point of land called Muskie Snout, on the south end. The other, on the north end, was smack on top of the eight-mile bar, an underwater ridge with drop-offs, deep ones, a good spot to angle for walleyes, and if you stayed close to shore on the east side you might get a poke at a long northern. Gun had taken a twenty-pounder there one year.

"Suppose you tell me what's going on between you and this Faust devil," said Jack. "Ha."

"I can't rightly say yet. He's acting like he knows more than he should know. He doesn't want to talk to me. He's got all his friends running interference. We'll just have to wait until it's face-to-face and hear what he's got to say. Could be, it's all just bile, plenty of that inside of him. Or maybe he's messed up in a murder."

"Where do you want to meet?" Jack asked.

"Say, Leo's Bait and Cafe? That place on the west side?"

"The one with the stop sign painted on the roof. That little guy with the eyes."

"That's it. How early can you leave?"

"Long as it takes me to get my fishing clothes on and gas up. Jack Knife's about halfway to the Cities, so if we leave now—let's see, it's seven—we'll both get there by nine or so. And Gun . . ."

"Yeah."

"Carol Long told me she's coming with us. Told me in a voice I don't argue with." He coughed. "In fact she's standing here right now."

"See you both, then," Gun said.

24

Gun got there first and made arrangements with the owner to rent two snowmobiles for the night. Leo was a guy so small you'd mistake him for a half-grown boy if you saw him from behind and didn't look too hard. His face was young, too, the absence of wrinkles almost shocking beneath the heavy thatch of white hair which he combed straight back and never covered with a cap, not even tonight at minus five, not counting windchill. His eyes were nearly the same color as his hair, icy gray, and you knew it when he looked at you. It was like being watched by a cat.

"Cold," said Gun.

"Warming, the weatherman says. Supposed to be up around twenty by morning. Kind of late to be going out, isn't it? Unless you've got yourself a shack." He waited for a moment, watching. "You got one?"

"No." Gun didn't feel like fabricating a story. Besides, the man probably needed some mystery in his life.

"You've got a friend on the way, then," said Leo. The two of them stood down at the rocky shoreline, just outside the long cement building where Leo kept his rental snowmobiles. The snow cover on Jack Knife was beautifully clean and the air so pure and hard from the cold that Gun felt it like a pressure against every surface of exposed skin: his face, and his hands now as he rolled a cigarette.

"A couple friends, and here they are now, looks like." The lake road cut between the shore and Leo's place, and Jack's Scout was pulling off into the gravel parking lot, headlights going black as he ground to a stop. He was out of the driver's door even before the Scout quit rocking on its lousy shocks.

"In a hurry, too," said Leo. His cool eyes were sheepish with curiosity.

Gun whistled and raised one hand, saw Jack and Carol look around, see him, and hunch themselves forward against the wind.

"A woman," said Leo.

"Is most of the spearing getting done on the upper or lower?" Gun asked.

"Upper, always. Course, some guys like the southern half, closer to town in case you run out of bottles." He almost grinned, but caught himself. "But mostly they're north. Same place as usual, east of the anglers. Though right now quite a few guys've got themselves off that little tit of land the DNR owns. Know where I mean?" Leo pointed toward the north. "There's just a few of 'em up there now, along the rushes stretching away from the bar." Leo turned to look at Jack and Carol, entering the circle of light cast by the yard lamp.

"Nice night to be on the lake, glad you thought of us," Jack said. In his red-and-black checked parka he looked comfortable and excited, his eyes like little pulsating bulbs.

"Thanks for coming." Gun turned toward Carol as he said it. "Hope you've got enough wool on underneath that thing. Jack's?"

Carol nodded. She wore green military coveralls too short in the limbs and stood with her arms out stiff from her body. "I don't think there's such a thing as enough."

"Leo's gotta gas up the machines, so we might as well go inside," Gun suggested. "Plan strategy."

In the wooden booth Carol sat next to Gun and under the table pressed her hand on his thigh. In the canvas military getup she smelled like cinnamon rolls in a burlap bag. Sweetness smothered. Jack said he was sure he'd recognize Faust by the photo which appeared with his column every day in the paper, and it was agreed that Jack would cover the lower lake, Gun and Carol the upper.

When Jack went to the men's room, Gun found himself not knowing what to say. He'd never felt like this with Carol before. He took her hand and said, "I've been thinking of you," aware of how weak it sounded.

"Wouldn't know it by the phone calls and post-cards."

"It's only been a few days."

"And you've been *so* busy, I know all about it. But Gun, I have a bad feeling, and I don't know exactly why. Is there something I should know about? Something you should be telling me?" The earnestness in Carol's dark eyes was disconcerting, but Gun didn't look away.

"I'll be real careful," he said.

"Lots of things can happen. Often they don't even seem dangerous at the time." Carol lifted her perfect chin. Her green eyes didn't challenge him, they were sad.

"I've always tried to learn from my mistakes, Carol. I've got a good long memory, you know that. . . ." But as he said it, he remembered Diane Apple's face, her hair, the sound of her voice, the way she possessed the small cabin by just lifting an arm.

"Thanks," said Carol. "I want you back here, soon."

Jack returned to the table and they all zipped up and went out into the crystal night air. It was so cold Gun felt his lungs lock up for an instant, his heart give a little extra push, gear down. At the lake Leo handed out helmets with plexiglass face bubbles and started both machines. "Save your heads from freezing, turning black, and falling off," he said.

"Au revoir," said Jack. He revved his engine and left in a cloud of oily exhaust, heading south. Gun and Carol started north, Gun at the helm, Carol perched on the back of the cushioned seat. The few lights in the distance came from the settlement of fish houses three miles off, small white lights nearly indistinguishable from the lowest stars, which tonight were especially crisp, reminding Gun of the tent he'd slept in as a kid, lying there at night, a full moon lighting up the pinholes in the canvas. By squinting he'd been able to make them twinkle and grow.

25

By the time they reached the edge of the fishing town Gun's fingers were numb. He wore a pair of sheepskin-lined choppers he'd borrowed from Jack, but holding on to the steel handlebars defrayed the insulating properties of the wool.

The little shack town looked much like the tract-house settlement where Clarence Coldspring lived, the main differences being snow instead of bare dirt for ground and a temperature ninety degrees colder. It was bigger, too. There were enough fish houses out here to cover a couple city blocks. Most of them were small, eight-by-ten or nine-by-twelve, but a few were more spacious, and a couple were nearly the size of a two-car garage. You could tell which ones were occupied by the smoke trails rising from the metal chimneys, the trucks or cars parked alongside.

Gun stopped the machine next to one of the larger fish houses, the outside done in cheap paneling, sitting at the edge of the settlement. On its side was a sign that said JIMMY BOONE, RT. 1, STONY, MN. "You as cold as I am?" he asked Carol.

"Not bad, really. I've got you in front of me."

"You *look* cold. Your lips don't want to move when you talk."

"I can't feel them."

"We'll warm up here," he said, nodding at the paneled fish house. "You know Jimmy, I bet."

"What's he doing way down here?"

"Daughter lives nearby."

Jimmy Boone was Stony's only barber and he still cut hair for under five bucks, still lathered and shaved your neck with a straight blade once he'd finished with the scissors. Every winter he closed down shop except for two days a week and devoted himself to fishing like a monk does to work and prayer. He was a man of habits, Jimmy was, most of them good ones. His taste for root beer was legendary, and he made it—strong and dark—in his basement in town, then gave it out free to the neighborhood children. He was long widowed but kept his house and yard like a fussy wife, everything just so. People claimed that his comings and goings, even on days when he wasn't working, were steady as a clock.

Gun knocked on his door and Jimmy opened it, smiling. He was over six-feet tall and athletic: broad shoulders, hips still narrow, even at seventy plus. He wore a gray mustache and his lined face had a few days of silver growth and his breath was sweet with root beer. His eyes were dark green as a spruce tree on a cloudy day. "It's warm in here. Get in," he said.

He settled Gun and Carol on a pair of canvas fishing seats next to his oil burner, dipped an aluminum cook-pan into his angling hole and set it on the stove. "Somehow I'm not thinking root beer for the two of you." He reached to a high shelf and brought down a jar of instant coffee, which he set quickly on the floor when his red-and-white bobber disappeared underwater. He grabbed the retreating line and brought it in hand over hand. A large black crappie broke surface and flopped on the fish house floor.

"It's been all day for this bugger," Jimmy said. With expert fingers he removed the hook, then rose to his feet and tossed the fish out the door onto the ice. "Water should be hot real quick now," he said.

Carol looked from the pan of lakewater to Gun, her eyes wrinkling at the corners.

"I'm getting fingers again." Gun wiggled them above the stove.

"And hurt like a son-of-a-gun, I bet. You're not fishing tonight, are you? What's going on? I heard you were down in Florida somewhere, and this here's a long jump from there."

Gun started a quick summary of Moses Gates and the recent killings in West Palm Beach, but Jimmy cut him off.

"I'm a barber, remember? I hear it all. I know what you're up to. What I don't get is why you're sitting out here tonight with me on the God blessed North Pole."

"Neil Faust is why I'm here. Know who he is?"
Jimmy nodded.

"I think he can help me—not that he wants to."
Jimmy touched his finger to the water on the stove,

said, "Ouch," and lifted the pan using a leather mitten for a pot holder. He poured the hot water carefully into two mugs that said JOHN DEERE in green letters on the side. He did this with delicate care, measuring with his eye to be sure both mugs were equally full. Then he added instant coffee, pinching it from the jar with his fingers and stirring with a long plastic hook remover. "Neil Faust likes to spear, you know. Normally puts his house up north of here off the DNR land."

"You haven't seen him?"

"Nope. But I know the northerns've been active even farther north, up around that reef. Another quarter mile or so. It shouldn't be that hard to find him, if he's here. Look for his shingle, and I think he drives a Wagoneer, red one. Last year he did."

Gun tried the coffee and found it not too bad, strong enough to override the flavor of freshwater fish. He saw Carol pretend to sip. Jimmy reached into the hole, between the floor and the ice, and brought up a dark bottle of root beer. "Don't like coffee myself," he said, and snapped off the cap on a bottle opener affixed to the wall.

"I appreciate the help." Gun lifted his coffee in thanks.

"One thing. You wanna be real careful on those snowmobiles tonight, up around that reef. Gets cold like this and funny things can happen. Ice slabs start fighting amongst themselves and pretty soon you got open water. If you go much beyond the last spear houses you'll see a big ridge in the ice, probably six, seven foot high and at least a hundred feet long. Either side of it might well be open water—even in this weather. Where one slab's buckled under. It's not so deep there, but deep enough to drown. Be careful of yourselves." His warning was supported by a deep booming that sounded far off and right beneath them at the same time, like underwater thunder. "Hear that?" said Jimmy. "That's the ice, that's power."

"We'll be careful," Gun said. He drank a little more of Jimmy's coffee, watched Carol pretend to drink more of hers, and they left.

Jimmy was right: Faust's icehouse was easy to find. Gun counted just ten shacks clustered here, and the one with a red Wagoneer had Faust's name and address printed neatly on its side, in adherence to state law. Gun memorized the address: 4567 Lucky Street, Robbinsdale. He killed the snowmobile's engine and took his mittens off to blow into his hands, which had already begun to numb up again. His fingers felt like bones with no muscle or skin or nerve.

"Why isn't he out here checking us out?" Carol whispered.

"Asleep, probably. Bet he's got a little bunk and everything. Lots of guys do."

They walked to the door and knocked. Inside, someone said, "Huh?" and then a sound like a pair of feet thumping against the floor. "Just a second. Who is it?"

"Warden," said Carol, stern. Gun smiled at her, squeezing her elbow.

Faust opened the door then. He wore a gray thermal undershirt and fatigue trousers that looked brand-new, glossy and stiff. No shoes. His eyes were squinting and swollen with sleep, then came open in a hurry. Gun thought of bothersome squirrels he'd caught in a live trap and how their eyes seemed incapable of blinking—perfectly round, and frosty with fear. Except Faust did blink, once, then slammed the door shut in their faces. Gun heard the locking bolt slide into place.

"Just let me get dressed," Faust called. "Let me get dressed, then we'll talk. Be right there." Through the plywood walls they heard Faust moving around, rustling into clothes. He was quiet for a few moments. The light came on. He opened the door. The parka he wore was white. The pistol he held was blue, blue steel.

26

"Get inside, inside," he said, stepping to his right. "I mean it, come on," snapping the pistol fast, like a Ping-Pong paddle. His nostrils twitched and he sniffed loudly, shook his head. He was like a man full of expanding gas—his squirrel eyes enormous, his face taught and round.

"All I want is to hear what you and Billy talked about," said Gun. "What the hell's wrong with you?"

"I don't know who you mean. I don't know any Billy. Now get in here." He was still waving the pistol, and Gun and Carol did like he said.

"On the phone, you said you hadn't told him anything. What did you mean?"

"Shut the hell up and sit down, both of you." He leveled the barrel of the gun at Carol's face and she lowered herself to the floor of the fish house. Gun knelt beside her.

"Neil. If you're in trouble maybe we can help," he said. "It's not like anybody's accusing you of anything. Nobody's saying *you* killed anybody."

"Shit, no," said Faust. "I don't"—his mouth got stuck in an inadvertent smile—"kill people."

"Then you're not doing yourself any good this way. Think," said Carol. "Think it out, you're a journalist. This won't help . . . whatever it is." Carol's voice was perfectly moderated, low and ripe with good sense, and Gun saw the muscles in Faust's jaw relax. "We're here to ask for your help, Neil. Maybe we can help each other. But we've got to talk first. *You've* got to talk."

"I don't have to do anything, damn it." Faust took a deep breath and pinched at the inner corners of his eyes. "Shit." The hand with the pistol started to come down.

Gun was just reaching for it when the ice boomed again, twice, like two shotgun blasts, and Faust came to life, brought the pistol back up. The pressure was there in his face again, behind his eyes, pushing them out like bullet tips.

"Okay, you're both staying here," he said. "I'm leaving, to get things straightened out. And don't try to come after me. Just stay here." He took a padlock from the shelf next to the door and stepped outside, slowly, holding the pistol on Gun as he moved. He shut the door. The padlock clicked into place.

A moment later the Wagoneer started, its tires spinning, catching hold. Gun threw himself into the door with his shoulder. It held, but felt vulnerable. He kicked it with the sole of a boot and the hinge side began to sag. One more kick and the door yawned open the wrong way.

Faust's taillights were still visible in the clear night as Gun yanked the pull cord on the snowmobile. "You wait, we can't catch him with both of us on here. I'll come back."

"You better! Gun—"

He waved and throttled all the way down, the noise of the engine drowning Carol's voice. He aimed the machine's twin skis between Faust's tire tracks, which cut through a snow cover of eight inches or so, with drifts up to a foot and a half. He watched the speedometer needle rise quickly to forty on the gauge, then fifty and finally sixty-five, all the while keeping the Wagoneer's taillights at the top of his vision. Then they were gone. Disappeared. Thinking of Jimmy's warning Gun released the throttle and the snowmobile slowed. He drove on cautiously, no red lights in front of him now. Soon he saw the ridge of ice.

As he came closer to it, Faust's tracks showed evidence of a slide to the right, toward the shoreline a hundred yards away. Evidently Faust had locked his brakes and cranked his wheel to the right, but too late, because his tracks went up and over the ice ridge.

Gun stepped from his machine and carefully approached the reef. It was about seven feet high and not so steep you couldn't climb up the side of it, like a pitched roof. His boots had plenty of grip, and he eased forward on all fours, took hold of the top and pulled himself up for a look.

Black water. A lot of it. A large ragged hole in a crust of new ice which covered an even larger break in the winter slab. And right in the middle, standing on top of his sinking red Wagoneer, Neil Faust. The truck was three-quarters submerged and going down fast. Fifteen feet of open water separated him from the reef—a long swim in this kind of cold.

"Hop in, stroke hard, I'll give you a hand up. There's nothing else to do," Gun said. He started maneuvering himself down to the water's edge. He could see that Faust had already been in the water. His wet clothes held close to his body and Gun saw in the bright moonlight that he was starting to shake from exposure. He didn't have long.

"Hurry up! Now. We'll get you back to the fish house, warm you up. Come on—we're at the pool, Holiday Inn."

Faust looked down at the water, just six inches from the top of the cab now, then slowly crouched to his knees. He turned to the west, where the lake extended for a good two miles, then to the east, where there were lights on shore. They looked very close in the cold air.

"Don't be a damn fool. You've got one choice— listen to me, damn it—and that's me. Unless you want to kill yourself, and it can't be worth that much. Come on, jump in, swim."

Faust opened his mouth but all that came out was the sound of teeth knocking together in a cold spasm.

"Jump, you idiot!"

Then the top of the Wagoneer disappeared with the sound of a giant watercooler releasing a bubble. Faust rose to his feet, looked down once at the lake rising above his ankles, turned toward shore and threw himself belly first into the water, away from Gun. It took him half a dozen sloppy strokes to reach the edge of the thin ice, which crumbled when he tried to haul himself on top of it. He struggled forward again but the ice wouldn't hold. His arms and legs were wild, sending icy water in all directions. His breath came in short loud gasps which vaporized in the air. He started to yell then, producing a ragged string of vowel grunts that sounded like the cow bear Gun had frightened on the Crow River one spring.

"This way!" Gun shouted. He felt sick at the bottom of his stomach, told himself he'd be crazy to go in after the man. It was too cold. He'd be as dumb as Faust—the guy would weigh three hundred pounds in that waterlogged gear he had on. *He's going to die, and I'm just watching.*

Gun started to remove his parka but then, miraculously, Faust was out of the water and lying on his belly on thin ice. He wasn't more than forty feet from the reef, and about the same distance from where the truck had gone down. Gun scrambled along the reef until he was opposite Faust, who wasn't moving at all now, just lying belly down, arms and legs spreadeagled. His eyes were closed.

"Stay put, I'm coming after you." Gun had his parka off, just in case, and he spread himself as thin as possible across the ice. From what he could tell it wasn't an inch thick, and he had no idea what he'd do once he reached Faust, but the man was in shock. The cold came right through his wool shirt and insulated underwear and told his brain to panic. *Now you'll die, too. Both of you. Wash up on shore during the spring melt, nicely preserved.* Gun bit his lip and started forward, keeping every possible inch of himself distributed upon the surface. *Stay on top, go slow.* He heard and felt the ice creaking beneath him, saw a picture of himself as a tiny insect caught in a huge glittering web, waiting. The ice snapped, released, held. He told himself to breathe. *Don't stop breathing, don't stop moving, don't do anything too fast.*

Ahead, Faust's eyes came open. They were all Gun could see inside the soaked parka hood, and they didn't reflect the situation. Behind the dull gloss of fear was sharp defiance that said, You don't have me.

Gun stopped moving. "Neil, listen to me. You've got to try and move this way. The ice will hold you. It's holding you now. Keep yourself flat and spread out and slide forward. Pretend you're a snake. Come on. You'll freeze there if you don't move."

Faust turned his head the other way toward the lights on shore, which were diffused into large blots by pine trees. Gun could see by the tightening and preparation in Faust's shoulders that he was going to try for the good ice—another forty or fifty feet away.

It wasn't any good trying to stop him, Gun knew that, but he tried anyway, sliding forward as fast as he dared, saying, "You can't make it that way, Neil. Don't even try."

Faust rose up on his hands and knees and started crawling away—he looked like a bug on water, he was moving so fast—going ten, twenty feet, then he was under the ice, out of sight without a struggle or a sound. Gun crept forward, watching for a hand, a face, a foot, anything, in the spot where Faust had disappeared, and when he neared the hole of open water he saw a shadow beneath the surface, dark and moving. He reached forward with one hand and stirred the water, felt nothing. He inched ahead until his face was above the hole. Peered down. Then the ice gave way and Gun was sucking a last gulp of air before the cold had him. He felt his clothes take on weight, the pull of gravity toward bottom, the icy, lost fear in his chest. But he didn't sink far. His feet found lake bottom in just seconds—*eight feet down?*—and he bent his knees, tried to recall his scattered wits back from the water which was drawing them away along with precious heat. He drove upward with every kind of strength he owned, eyes wide open, passing a closed fist on his way, broke surface and sucked his chest full. He blinked the water from his eyes and felt already the reluctance of his muscles to respond to his brain. Blinking was conscious work. There wasn't time for anything. There wasn't time for Neil Faust. But Gun made one more trip below, thinking, *Look for the fist and take hold of it, grab it.*

Faust was floating like a balloon in a soft breeze about three feet off the bottom, his face surprised in the parka hood, mouth slack, eyes cracked wide. Gun, out of air, pushed once more for the top and when he got there knew he didn't have a choice. He started a hard crawl toward the reef, bringing his hands down like hammers on each stroke, smashing the ice, then following through with his body, the sound ringing in his ears like glass. He reached the ice reef and tried to find a hold on it, but it slanted up too steeply, giving him nothing. His fingers could just as well have been someone else's for all the good they did him. He edged his way along the reef until he came to a flat spot where he could plant his elbows and hoist himself chest high. For a few seconds he rested in that position, most of him dangling in the water, his arms and chest and head freezing fast in the cold air. He closed his eyes, trying to will his nerves and muscles into obedience beyond the cold, then leaned forward and pushed down against the ice, rolling to the side as he came out of the water.

Nothing was left in Gun's mind except an image of a tiny little fellow, cold and wet and clinging to the inside of his shirt, shivering against his chest—so small he could fit in a shirt pocket but fully grown nonetheless and his fingers like mouse fingers clutching to Gun's skin. Gun curled himself around his small passenger and scrambled over the top of the reef and slid down the other side, where he saw an eternity of sand. Long dunes, wind fashioned, sunbaked.

Knowing he was safe, Gun lay down to sleep.

27

He woke to a pain he knew from childhood. Frostbitten skin thawing. Coming in from a late afternoon of trapping muskrats on the bay, reaching into cold water to reset the steel-jawed traps, his fingers and toes and ears and face all aching with a deep urgency that said, You're lucky we're still here.

First just that feeling, and the awareness of being dry and warm, itchy all over. A wool Hudson Bay blanket—red, white, and green—wrapped tightly around him. Then Carol's face, glowing, her eyes calm, lips tight with concern. And above her a small gold cross tacked to a plywood wall, and the words HOPE FOR ALL.

"How's your fingers and toes feel?" The mouth that entered Gun's vision was mostly covered by a gray mustache going yellow with age. "They tingle some? Or more than that?" asked Jimmy Boone.

"More than that," Gun said. "Feel like they're going to blow up here any second. Bratwurst on the grill."

"They'll be fine. Give 'em an hour. They weren't even white yet, you just had a little case of the hypothermia comin' on. We get it warm enough in here?"

Gun realized Jimmy had a large drop of sweat ready to fall from his generous nose. He looked at Carol, whose face was dotted with moisture, each particle relaying a small bit of the light cast by Jimmy's gas lantern.

"How'd you get me here?" Gun asked her.

"I had some help." Carol took Gun's hand and with a little too much pressure began to stroke it. "That reef's close by, like Jimmy said. When you stopped the snowmobile I could still see the headlight, so I ran. Then Jimmy . . . happened along?" She looked up at the old man.

"I had this here feeling about things," Jimmy said, "so I took a little drive up that way. But she didn't need me. Time I showed up, she had you practically draped over the back of that Ski-Doo."

Gun freed his arms from the blanket, ruining the tuck, and gripped the edge of the cot he was on. He pulled himself to a sitting position. He saw his clothes strung up above the hot stove, and it wasn't until then, seeing his pants and shirt and long johns hanging there empty and damp, that he remembered Faust.

"Couldn't get him out," Gun said. "He had on that parka—the water was so damn cold."

"You were lucky to get yourself out," said Carol. She stood and pressed her palms against Gun's chest until he eased himself back down on the cot. Her expression was steady and patient. "Thank God," she said.

"So, what did Faust go over the reef for?" Jimmy asked, matter of fact. He was stirring a teaspoon of coffee into boiled lakewater, deliberate.

"I've never seen a man like that, so scared," Gun said. "He wasn't going to talk to me if it killed him."

"Which it did," said Jimmy.

"He wouldn't let me help him. You wouldn't believe it. I could've tossed the guy a rope, he'd have tossed it back."

"Whatever he did, or whatever he knew, it's pretty safe now," said Carol. "What next?" She took the coffee from Jimmy and handed it to Gun.

"Drive to Minneapolis and have a look through his house. Do you know what time it is?"

"Midnight—ah, twelve-thirty," said Jimmy, checking his pocket watch.

"So you're not planning on telling anybody what happened tonight," said Carol, her eyes grim. She pushed her dark bangs straight back from her forehead and took a long breath.

"No, I'm not." Gun drank the coffee carelessly, burning his tongue and throat. He felt the heat flash through his lungs like a light. "Nobody up here knows a thing about this situation and they'd have me answering questions for a week. I won't do that. I can't."

"Gun, we can't just leave him under there."

Jimmy cracked open a root beer on the bottle opener, which was Hamm's-Beer-blue and shaped like a cartoon bear. He took a long pull from the chipped brown bottle.

"There's a man under the ice, dead, and he's got a family, friends. It's not right to leave him there, even if you think it *is*. Even if you've got important things to do." Carol accepted a cup of coffee from Jimmy but kept her eyes on Gun. He looked away from her, then back, unwilling to accept the guilt she was pushing.

"Under normal conditions, there's also the matter of your Ski-Doo tracks, and Faust's tracks, and whether they'd be able to piece together anything from them," said Jimmy. "But the weather's going to cure you of that worry." He stood up and held aside the curtain from the small window to reveal a dark square of falling snow. "What I can do is make a little call to the sheriff in the morning. Almore's an old friend of mine. I just call him and say I heard a little shouting in the night, north of here, and I go to have a look but it's snowing pretty good and I don't dare get too close to that reef. I tell him maybe he should go up there and have a look. And he'll be able to see how the ice has been busted up and refrozen."

Jimmy turned to Carol and nodded solemnly. "I don't want to think about a man under the water. Faust can be under there"—Jimmy pointed down with his thumb—"or underneath a carved stone, and it doesn't make a whisper of difference at this point. Not to him, at least."

He stood up and slapped at Gun's pants hanging above the stove. "Coming along," Jimmy said.

"Won't be but another half hour." He took another swallow, smacked his lips, and gave a little wave with his bottle of root beer. "Now this batch here, it's got a little spark to it," he said.

28

At two A.M. Gun was driving his rented car south toward Minneapolis and not feeling too bad, considering. He had the heater going full bore, a large insulated mug of coffee on the dashboard and a cigarette rolling on one knee. His fingers and toes were tender but free of pain now, and his body had the kind of all-over soreness a guy feels about two days after a home-plate collision. He wasn't coughing or sneezing. In fact, there was nothing bad in his chest, only a sympathetic catch whenever he thought of how cold he'd been just two hours ago.

Once his clothes had dried enough to put back on, he and Carol had driven the snowmobile back to Leo's, which was closed up. They found Jack in his truck in the parking lot, half asleep and half frozen. He listened to their story, unimpressed as usual, then asked two questions. First, was Gun going to let anyone know about Neil Faust? Gun explained what Jimmy Boone was going to do in the morning. Second, Jack wanted to know, could he go home to bed now?

"Not that I've done a blessed thing. But if it's all the same to you, I'm ready to call it a night." He was behind the wheel of his truck, and Gun and Carol shared the wide seat with him. "In fact," he said, "I might tap you to drive us back, Carol. You seem a little perky, still. I'm afraid I'd just run us off the road."

Gun told Jack thanks and kissed Carol good-bye, once on the mouth and once on the forehead. With his thumb he smoothed away the vertical lines there. Then he got out of the truck and watched them pull away, north toward Stony. He was still standing in the parking lot when Jack's Scout came to a stop fifty yards up the road and Carol and Jack switched places. But then instead of moving forward, the truck backed up until it was next to Gun again. Carol, in the driver's seat, rolled down her window. She said, "My grandpa always did that, kissed me on the forehead before I left."

"I like your forehead."

"You're not my grandpa, though."

"True enough, and I'm grateful for that."

"Gun, I'm glad you're all right. I don't know what I'd do . . ." Carol wasn't a woman who cried, but the shake in her chin did some damage to Gun's control. He clenched his jaw and swallowed, then reached for her face.

"Now leave the right impression, or I'm not going anywhere," Carol said.

He leaned down and took his time with the kiss, thinking, Remember this when you see Diane Apple.

Neil Faust's address was easy to find, just a few blocks off Highway 81 in a neighborhood of large older homes and mature trees. Gun parked a block north and approached the house by way of the alley.

There was no fence to block his way, and plenty of light to work by, thanks to a gas lamp in the backyard. No neighbors to worry about, either; the house was separated from those on both sides by tall evergreen hedges. He simply walked up to the rear porch, broke the window of the door with a mittened hand, and unlocked it. Inside, he jimmied a storm window with his pocket knife, then hoisted on the sash, popping its lock. Crawling through onto a white corduroy couch, he told himself he should really spend some time learning the finer points of breaking and entering. It made him uncomfortable, wrecking things like this. The point was to get inside, not advertise that you'd been there.

He searched quickly, using the small flashlight he'd picked up on the drive down at an all-night gas and grocery along with a quart of buttermilk and a ham and cheese. The first floor gave nothing. The telephone stand held a small Rolodex but it seemed to have been weeded. Not more than a dozen names were left, all of them local sports or news figures. On the second floor Gun found a study, two walls of books and two covered by photographs of a smiling Neil Faust posing with various jocks, mostly Twins and Vikings from past and present. Kent Hrbek, Kirby Puckett, Harmon Killebrew, Tony Oliva, Herschel Walker, Fran Tarkenton. Also Greg LeMond, and a mammoth-size, bald George Foreman. No Moses Gates, though. And no Rott Weiler.

A careful look through the desk produced nothing of interest except for a small brass key that opened an oak file cabinet in the bedroom one door over. There Gun found an unorganized nightmare of old check stubs, tax forms, utility and credit card bills, insurance records. He didn't spend long sorting through it all, but just before he gave up, he came across a notebook he couldn't pass up, a small one, the kind reporters took notes on, and this one had only a few pages filled. There were names of resorts and hotels, mostly in the Caribbean, and next to each name, food- and service-rating quotations from a travel guide. There were tentative flights and dates, cost calculations. And on the inside cover of the notebook was written FUNDS FOR FUN IN THE SUN, much embellished with an ink pen, and followed by a phone number with a Florida prefix. Gun tore out the page and stuck it in his wallet. He made a cursory search through the rest of the house before leaving.

At the Minneapolis–St. Paul Airport, he bought a nonstop flight for West Palm Beach, then found a phone. He dialed the Florida number and waited five rings for someone to pick it up.

"Yeah, Casper's place," a woman said.

"Casper?"

"That's what I said, didn't I? Who is this, anyway?"

"Casper *Johnson?*" Gun said, fishing.

The woman laughed at him. "Pal, you got the wrong Casper. Adios, now."

29

When Gun woke up the wheels of the Boeing were just hitting the runway and the white glare of Florida was coming in all over. Sleeping in the air was a talent he'd learned flying around the American League those seventeen years—trust the plane, let it hum you to sleep, turn on the overhead air and aim it at your eyelids. He'd got on the plane needing the rest and used it to forget Neil Faust for a while. Awake now he had Neil with him again, and when the big door opened and warm ocean air washed into the plane he had Harold Ibbins there, too, and Miss Mary. He got up and out with his duffel bag and the heavy air stuck to his skin like flies.

* * *

At the motel he took a long warm shower. He heard the phone ringing and thought, Let it wait.

It waited half an hour.

"Gun Pedersen," he said into the phone.

"I've been trying to get ahold of you all for two days here. Name's Pastor Floyd Wedfield, Harristown, Pennsylvania? I understand you're inquiring after a Weiler." The man spoke quickly for a southerner, and his voice was high and confident.

"That's right, Pastor," Gun said. "Thanks for—"

"Which one exactly you want to hear about?" he asked. "Lots of Weilers and Weiler relations, some of them following fairly clean lines and others awful muddied up, you know what I mean? Ever hear of that song, 'I'm My Own Brother's Dad and My Sister Calls Me Uncle'?"

"Can't say I have."

"But you get the idea."

Gun said, "Robert Weiler's the one I'm wondering about. I just wanted to know if you remember him and whether you knew his parents."

"I knew him and I know them. You make it sound like they're buried already."

"Aren't they?"

"Oh, they might wish they were, some days. Sam's got a bad old pump that puts him to bed every few weeks and Almona's hands are curled up like crabs from writin' letters to her kids, but I guess for their age that's not so bad."

"We're talking Rott's parents now?" Gun asked. "Robert Weiler: Minnesota Twins, San Francisco Giants, Philadelphia—"

"Biggest thing ever happened to Harristown, Pennsylvania. Biggest head ever to come forth from between a woman's thighs."

"Rott told me his parents were dead," Gun said.

"He always figured he deserved better than what he got himself born into. That sort of kid, that sort of man. I don't think his folks've seen him in a decade. Longer. And they still live in the same board shack on the same rented land. No phone or flush pot."

"He'd have you believe he comes from Civil War generals, old plantations, slaveholders. Cotton money."

"Well, now. There *is* money someplace. Not here, mind you, but somewhere. Rumor's got it that some relations—don't ask me what kind or when—moved down to Florida and got rich there—and don't ask me how, neither. I can't begin to guess."

Gun thought about Rott's farm and the year it was built. "Any way I could talk to his parents?"

"I'm not even gonna tell them you called. These people don't need to hear what you've got to say, and what could they tell you anyway? Look, Robert's got them killed in his mind, and I think they've finally let him die in theirs. Can't we just leave it like that?"

He stopped at the *By-Line* office on the way to Indiantown. Taylor Johns met him at the entrance and led him up the stairs and into her office with a stern briskness that made him feel he was about to be reprimanded. Closing the blond-wood door on the cubicle maze she put her back to it and faced him.

"Don't misunderstand me," she said. "I appreciate the tip. Billy would've appreciated it more. He worked that way."

Gun tried not to put anything on his face she could read.

"All our experienced reporters were tied up. I was showing our new kid around when I got your message about the Ibbinses." She was pretending to look around the room, but the corner of an eye was always on him. He said nothing. She said, "He was promising. The new kid. Straight out of a Tallahassee classroom, but he smelled a story and volunteered to go out and get it. He wanted to make front page on his first day."

"Ambitious," Gun said.

"Not anymore. Now he's in therapy, asking his analyst whether he should join the Peace Corps or sue his alma mater for educating him in a field so jolting to his psyche. He found them," she said, "just as you must have. Kid on his first story. Do you know, after we went to press, how many people wanted the identity of the mysterious tipster?"

"What did you tell them?"

"The truth. That we didn't have a name." She came away from the door and somehow summoned enough height to look Gun in the eye. "I don't know why you were out at the Ibbins place, but I'm sure it's because of Billy's Moses Gates crusade. No. I don't want to know. But you're doing things just how Billy would've done them, and look where it got him."

She subsided like a slow echo and gave him his first chance to say why he'd come. He pulled a folded *By-Line* clipping from his pocket.

"Why'd you run this last week?"

She squinted forward, took the clipping. "The Faust editorial." She sighed. "It's infuriating. Not at all what Billy would've liked."

"So why run it?"

"Not my decision. It's a local issue, so the Op-Ed people look for interesting angles on it. This *is* the sort of thing that gets readership."

"It's inflammatory, it's misinformed—" he began.

"Yes, yes," said Taylor Johns, a bit of hard business coming into her face, "and it's also, in a way, what kept me from telling the cops you tipped us the Ibbins story. I'd forgotten that when Billy first pitched me this Moses Gates thing, he showed me a sample of the sort of hatchet job some of the writers did on Gates back in seventy-seven. Trial by press, he said, and in retrospect that's just what it was." She had a file drawer open and was prospecting intensely, her fingers scissoring through newsprint. She slowed, plucked a file. "Look."

It was a photocopy of an old *City Beat* editorial. Minneapolis, 1977. The heading in bold capitals read simply FAUST, with a photo of smug Neil over the letters. Above the picture a teaser:

Columnist Reveals Source, Motive

Orlando—Watch. They're going to call it a suicide.

Three nights ago Jerry Gammer, who locks up Tinker Field when our Minnesota Twinkies are through with practice, was making a last check of the stadium when he found outfielder Ferdie Millevich hanging by a power cord from the press box. The discovery understandably caused violent distress to Mr. Gammer's digestive system, and has in fact unsettled the rest of baseball society as well.

Here's why I, for one, am feeling queasy.

In recent weeks, this column has taken more than a casual glance at the preseason fire storm that is the Minnesota Twins' training camp. You, faithful reader, have been treated to a major-league display of internal combustion, which is good for engines but not baseball teams. And things overheated.

It started when a Twins player began speaking out in this space about problems that've pestered the Minnesota organization for years. He spoke on the condition of anonymity, and some of the things he said put both the front office and the other players on edge. He said: 1) that Twins' owner Calvin Griffith regularly does other than he says during contract negotiations, 2) that Cal is a practicing bigot who's wanted for years to trade that uppity

Rod Carew, and 3) that several key players have said they're going to lie back this season and not play all-out, since it's plain old Cal will just trade them anyhow if they start, somehow, to win.

You can see why the player wanted anonymity. None of what he said was exactly new to people who know the Twins, but none of it was very nice, either. It doesn't matter now, because the player's name was Ferdie Millevich, and he is dead.

It's this prophet's guess we're going to hear that poor Ferdie was so unhappy that he did himself in. Don't believe it.

It's no writer's duty to project doubt on the innocent, but read on and see if you don't think a little projecting is in order here. This spring I've spent more time in the clubhouse with Our Gang than the *Beat* or any other decent paper would pay me for, and the word for the way Ferdie got treated I'd get spanked for using. The trouble with being an anonymous source is that it's hard to stay anonymous. Things tend to get loose in clubhouses. Things like who's bad-mouthing whom. Ferdie might have thought he had a secret, but the Twins knew.

It showed in how they talked to him. Once upon a time there was gladness in the Twinks' clubhouse; they seemed to be happy with themselves even if nobody else was. Not this spring. Walk in after practice and you better have your chain mail on because everybody is in a biting mood, and it seemed like Ferdie Millevich was bleeding the most. You want incidents? Think. Who was it shortstop Donny Miner threatened to take a piece of moments after the Twinks' first spring-training loss to Cincinnati? Ferdie Millevich. Who's locker was humorlessly packed with a fresh load of junk straight from the dairy-barn floor? Ferdie's. And what was it

our own venerable catcher, Mr. Moses Gates, had to
say after reading the first of our "nameless source"
columns?

What was that, Moze?

If memory serves, and it usually does, Moses said
the troublemaker we were quoting ought to be
strung up. *Strung up.*

Don't mind me, folks. I'm just doing a little
projecting. Thinking out loud while we wait for the
coroner's report.

If they say suicide, I'm gonna be sick.

"To be nailed like that," said Taylor Johns, seeing
him finish, "without defense. It's unimaginable. Billy
was absolutely right. Moses never lost the shadow."

Gun breathed deeply. Reading the old column had
sunk him right back in the wreck of 1977. And his
own, three years later. He felt old shards of anger
working through, anger at the thing in people that
always wanted to know the worst, or make it up
when necessary. He said, "So. Why didn't you tell
on me?"

When she answered it was softly. "Because Billy
was right, and because you're doing it just as he
would've."

"And look where it got him," Gun said.

"Yes. Be careful."

He told her he would, of course, and going out into
the uncomplicated Florida sun he let a little of the
anger go off from him. Because, he remembered, there
was Diane to see, and Neil Faust for all his nastiness
was drifting in a deeper, colder Hell than he'd ever
hoped to grace.

Diane had chilled the wine he'd bought at Cliffert's
but they didn't feel much like drinking it.

"You've been to *Minnesota?*" she asked. She wore a
pale yellow skirt cut full and a loose white blouse.

She'd freed her hair from the braid and some of it blew forward over her shoulders like a cinnamon breeze. The deck of the *Long Napper* was soaped and glowing in the sun slant.

"There was a man there I had to talk to. Newspaper man," Gun said.

"About Moses? Or Billy?"

"Both. This was one of the guys who made things hard for Moses back when Ferdie Millevich died. Jumped on him like he'd seen Moses do the deed himself." He shook his head. "Columnists with a grudge make you wonder pretty hard about freedom of the press."

"You, especially," she said.

He'd imagined that Diane didn't know enough of his background to understand his dislike of journalists. Some journalists. He saw her smiling at him and there was some new comprehension in her face, a grasp of him that had not been there before; but there was the smile, too, and so he smiled back and said, "Me, especially."

"Did he know Billy?"

Gun leaned his head back and followed the line of the *Napper*'s mast with his eyes. He still felt grimy and thick with all the travel and what he had to tell her wasn't going to improve things.

"Diane, he more than knew him. I think he gave your brother the information that killed him."

She leaned forward. "He told you this?"

"No. But I think he was the guy Billy had just come back from seeing before he was murdered."

"Wait—"

"It's what Moses said. That your brother called him that night saying he'd just gotten back, that he'd gotten the big break on the story. I think Faust was the break."

"Billy's last interview," she said. She was soft for a moment and then was on her feet, stalking around the deck. "I never actually believed it. That he died because of some broken-down ballplayer he felt sorry for. It just didn't seem right, not when there were so many stories out there that were so much more— more threatening." She spoke faster, pacing. "You talked to this Faust? What did he *say?* Listen, I'm going tonight, to Minnesota I mean—"

"There's no need," Gun said quietly.

She stopped and stood facing him with the sun behind her hair.

"Faust's dead."

She backed to the rail and gripped it, the fingers going white with pink half dimes beneath the nails.

He said, "I never got to talk to him. We were out on the ice, he was trying to lose me."

She didn't say anything. It was hell to explain.

"The ice broke. I couldn't reach him."

Diane turned and looked over the water. Gun came near her and the wind brought her hair back until a few strands of it touched his arm. She was so quiet Gun didn't know she was crying until she spoke and it was in her voice. "I can't get used to this," she said. "All these people dying."

They got around to the wine at last. The sun was gone and clouds were racking up low, covering the stars. A breeze came in over the palms smelling of rain. They were still on deck, a little too cool and liking it after the day's heat. The wine was white and cold and tickled a little going down.

"It's good," Diane said. In the clouded moonlight the whites of her eyes looked pale blue next to her deep brown irises.

He said, "Cliffert recommended it."

"I drove into West Palm today. Looked you up in the library."

"I wasn't in the library."

"Yes, you were." It was getting darker. He was losing the whites of her eyes. "That was some stir you made back in eighty, quitting the team. I don't know where I was hiding."

"In the right place, apparently."

In the darkness a glow of a smile. "And then you just . . . went off? Disappeared into the boreal forest?"

"It's quiet there. Usually."

"I like quiet, too," she said.

They had some, and it was easy as the wine, and Diane said, "You never married again."

"No."

"You must have someone. Up north."

He nodded, knowing she could not see him.

There was a moment when the moon had its last chance and lit up the night for the space of two breaths, and Gun saw her looking at him and behind her the lunar incandescence hitting the water and silver masts of the marina. When the clouds shut them back into blackness Diane rose without a word. He heard her breath sweep past him close and imagined without effort the coolness of her legs beneath the skirt. She went below, stepping easily down into darkness then lighting a lamp that put a shimmer of yellow out on the water.

He sat upon the deck smelling the green palms and rain off somewhere between himself and the coast, and it seemed to him that spoken invitations had always been the easiest to resist. A gust snapped at his hair and the boat pulled gently against itself in the slip, and the yellow light shining gave him a sudden joy like an anchor coming unmucked at last. He stood and holding the rail followed after Diane. Then finally Carol Long came into his principled brain with her contrary mind and her bright black hair, and he knew he didn't have room inside for two and made his choice.

He stepped off the boat slowly so as not to rock it and thought he was clear when Diane's voice called "Gun?" and there was fear in it.

"Here," he said.

She came up from below, light rising around her in the open hatchway. She still wore the skirt and yellow blouse but there was something wrong in her face. Gun stepped back aboard and went to her.

"It's Billy," she said. She held a single playing card and he saw the staring Queen of Diamonds. "It was here all the time," she said simply. "He's left something for me."

30

It was the notes, she was sure of it, Billy's missing interviews, though they searched the *Long Napper* until her giddiness at finding the card turned to stiff resolve. She made them do it all again, she starting from the aft stateroom and he from the cramped space forward, working over and under and between the cushions and stowed life vests, emptying and refilling the dozen Chock Full O' Nuts coffee cans in the moldy bilge where Billy tucked spare blocks and cleats. When they met in the middle of the boat her eyes looked muddy and her skirt mistreated.

"This much shouldn't happen in one evening," she said, sitting.

"It's morning." The galley clock said 12:15.

"Good morning. There's nothing down here, is there?"

Gun shook his head. "We could go up top. Maybe he stashed them on deck somewhere." But his voice was tired and he knew she heard it.

"You're thinking I'm wrong, aren't you?" she said. Looked that way.

"That the card is nothing. Maybe it was sitting around for years, maybe he hid it before I came three, four visits ago and I just never found it."

"Maybe."

She'd crossed her legs and was swinging the top one back and forth like some sort of mainspring that would fuel the rest of her, feed her energy, wind her up. Standing again she gave a short urgent laugh. "Maybe, yes," she said, not meeting his eyes, "but wouldn't it be bitchy weather if we were wrong?"

The luck on deck was lousy. They didn't split up but worked side by side with a flashlight, Diane jean-jacketed and chilled as mist formed around them on the water. His knees on the hard deck, his fingers feeling every inch of teak, Gun had the embarrassing sense that he'd regressed into boyhood and was looking again for some mouldering chest of gold. It had been much more fun back then. Something about being six years old, and believing there was something to find.

Still, Billy had believed enough in boyhood and danger to build a cache in his bathroom at home; and so they worked the deck, took the seats out of the cockpit, removed the huge old sentimental captain's wheel from its spindle and shined the flashlight on it. When the boat was wrecked to Diane's angry satisfaction she said, "The mast," and they took it down, lowering it straight aft on what Diane called the tabernacle until it rested back over the transom. It was a wood mast and hollow and the big bronze halyard block at the tip pried off easily. They aimed what they could of the flashlight beam inside but there was nothing.

They righted the mast and she sat with her back against it and her legs crossed, her mainspring now not moving at all.

"In the morning," Gun said, "we can talk about what to do." He had the flashlight and was playing it idly over the boat in the neighboring slip.

"It's morning," she reminded him.

The boat next door was a fine old sportfisherman that stood up high-shouldered from the water. It was white with the lower hull gone reddish from too many seasons without cleaning. It had classic ring portholes in tarnished bronze.

"It isn't right," she said absently. "I found the card, there should be something on the boat. In the boat—"

The old sportfisherman had a rail around its forward deck, draped with a tangle of chain and rope, and a folding navy anchor hung over the side.

"Or outside the boat," she said. Gun saw that she was looking at the anchor. Thinking.

"I didn't see one when we were looking. An anchor."

"Of course not," she said. "It's in the water."

"Here in the marina? Why? The boat's secure, all tied up."

She led the way forward slowly enough to let him know she wasn't getting her hopes up and they found the chain exiting its worn hole, swinging down loosely into the water.

The power winch was disconnected and Gun had to lean down and grasp the cold links and pull the anchor up hand-over-hand. It was a straight mushroom-shaped thing of perhaps forty pounds with a clean wide shaft and a bellyful of silt. Gun knelt and studied it in the white beam and there circling the shaft was a slender even crack not an inch from the top, and he knew the six-year-old was about to find his treasure.

31

He wedged the anchor between his knees and screwed the top off like it was a mason jar.

The preserves were even better than they'd hoped for.

"The interviews," Diane breathed. She was holding the light on a rubber-banded Baggie Gun had extracted from the anchor. Inside were a narrow steno pad, the cardboard cover inked solid with names and telephone numbers, and two tape cassettes the size of cigarette lighters.

She'd seen Billy's little Sony in the glove box of the Lincoln and was back on the boat with it in the time it took Gun to unwrap the Baggie and take it below. The tapes were unlabeled. He looked at the notebook cover while she tried to figure out the recorder. Rott Weiler's name was there. Harold Ibbins. Neil Faust. A list of others he didn't know.

"Ohh-kay, we're testing one-two-three," said all that remained of Billy Apple.

Diane's jaw was clenched knuckle-white.

"It's, what, eleven-thirty at night, second of January 1991, and we're talking *live*"—Billy's voice suddenly turning top-40—"from high atop the emergency ward at St. Luke's Sickhouse in West Palm Beach. Here we are in the waiting room and I'm finding out why they call it that. The day after New Year's, can you believe this?"

Diane didn't look like she could. The voice on the tape was strong and round and there was humor in it, but also tiredness and pain.

"As of now, Moses Gates owes me one hell of a favor," Billy said, his breathing noticeably short. There was a lull and a shuffling, some nearby activity in the waiting room, and the voice went to a whisper and lost its humor. "For the record. I turned in before the news tonight. Sick stomach, Pepto Pukehole. I'm barely asleep and then headlights are coming in my bedroom window. Nervous . . . I got up and looked out and somebody's parked out in my oranges. Piss me off? And they wouldn't turn their lights off. So I went to the door, in my Jockeys. I opened it and they were right there . . . God what a sick stomach, and then seeing these two. The big one I'm already having nightmares about, he's hunched forward all the time and seems built wrong, the way hyenas are built wrong, all shoulders but God how big and crafty . . . I thought, oh shit I wrote the wrong thing and they had me all right, said nothing, they hauled me back to their van—that's right, you pricks, I wasn't too scared to notice your sweet little Ford van—they dragged me back there and got a rope off the backseat. Intro to Journalism . . . the big one tossed the rope up and I thought, You know these trees are probably just barely big enough to hang from. He makes a loop for my neck . . . God damn them, this isn't two hours ago! The smaller one says, 'You want to live?' Well, sure. 'Okay then,' he says, 'you go on to the next big scoop and let Moses Gates go down to Hell.' And the big one takes the rope and makes a knot like a fist and clubs me right in the sick gut with it until I puke my supper at his feet. And they went away."

Diane stopped the tape. She'd been crying through it but had quit now and was only drawn. "It's like it's not him," she said. "He's—tough."

"Yes."

She clicked the Sony on again. "Still waiting," said Billy. "Feeling better. Bruised ribs is all, I bet." The voice rising and getting back its roundness. "Ford Aerostar, and I know the plates. Plates now, names tomorrow. This is what I went to school for, you bastards, and you should've just strung me up because one sunny morning, sooner than you think, I'm going to get out of bed and screw your lives."

When she put up her hands to cover her eyes Gun saw the prickles on her forearms.

32

The Aerostar was registered to Casper Leavitt. Billy got to that on side two of the same tape after detailing his bruises and two cracked ribs. Gun remembered calling the number he'd found in Faust's file cabinet, the girl saying, "You got the wrong Casper."

A street mugging, Billy had told the doctor. He told the truth to a friend at law enforcement who traced the plates. And then went out and learned everything he could about Leavitt, most of it from Clarence Coldspring.

"You want to talk, man, you put that thing away,"

they heard Clarence say on tape. "Those things, they make me sound like a wuss." That was it from Clarence, but there were some notes in Billy's pointy scrawl in the steno pad that went over what Gun and Diane already knew: the night raids, the disappearances of Coldsprings over the years, the bones in the swamp. Billy came back on the tape and narrated a minute or so of what he knew about Casper Leavitt: that he'd been a big dairy man, sold off in the government buyout, that he gave generously to the senate campaign of a former Klan official, who lost anyhow. Nothing surprising.

It was running toward three in the morning and with the adrenaline going dry Gun felt slow, almost underwater. He looked at Diane over the Sony and she said, "There's the other tape."

Harold Ibbins didn't remember a single sinister thing about the day Ferdie Millevich died, though Billy tried hard to make him.

"It was a lousy day for practice, is what it was," Ibbins mused. "All around. Night before, there were gale warnings on the coast, the forecast was for rain, so me and Gates and some others went out after curfew and put a few down. More than a few. Then next day the damn skies cleared up"—Ibbins gave a husky chuckle—"so Skip called an afternoon practice. Practice? Man, we couldn't even *see.*"

Billy said, "Was Rott Weiler with you? Putting 'em down?"

"Rott? Man, no. He was so sure of practice getting scrapped that he went down to see some lady in Miami. That was Rott. Probably still is. I was sitting with my head in a sling and he called me up to find out was there practice. Damn right, I say, and I'm gonna see three baseballs for every one comes my way, and where the hell're you? He giggles a little and he says

I'm in the Hotel Miami, or what-the-hell-ever, and I'm not even gonna open the *shades* till tomorrow morning, you think of something to tell the Skip."

"When did he get back?"

"Next day, I guess. After they found Ferdie. Rott, you know, he wasn't so brokenhearted about it."

Long silence from Billy. Finally, "You roomed with Rott for a while. What did he think of Ferdie Millevich?"

Ibbins chuckled again. "Think of him? Listen. Ferdie was starting to swing the bat, you know? He was comin' around, and playing some good outfield. Only he wasn't a regular, like Rott was. Last part of seventy-six, Rott went into a hell of a slump, he was like one-for-thirty-four, and the manager, Mauch, tells Rott to sit down and up gets Ferdie. And Ferdie hits about four-fifty for the last twelve games of the year. Rott wonders, Do I have a job? See, that's what he thought of him." Harold took a couple breaths that sounded like tough ones and his voice took on some gravel. "Actually, it went deeper than that. Stop the tape."

There was a clicking and Ibbins was back. Either Billy had talked him into staying with the recorder, or Harold didn't know it was still on.

"Look at me, now," Ibbins said.

"What about you."

"I look as white as you, don't I? Sure. But I've got black in me, on my mother's side. One-quarter black, give or take a squirt. Tell you what, me and Rott were just fine until we're up late one night in Anaheim and I let it go, about my blood. Throw him? Like a damn catapult. It chewed on him good and finally we had a big blowout in the clubhouse, and after that he started staying with Ferdie on the road. Now *there* was a match made in heaven, two guys going after the same job—"

"Why'd they do that? Who assigned rooms?"

"Rott asked Ferdie, far as I know. Ferdie said okay."

"They get along, then?"

"Uh-uh. I think what happened, Ferdie found out about the badness between Rott and me. Old Millevich, he was a Minnesota boy, you know? Read Dr. King, a real abolitionist. Let me tell you something about Rott Weiler. The only thing he hates more than blacks is whites who don't hate blacks."

"Well," Diane said, "what do we know?" The galley table was littered with cassettes, Billy's papers, muddy-bottomed coffee cups. It was three-thirty A.M. and even the light seemed old.

"Rott hated Ferdie, and somebody paid Faust to set Ferdie up," Gun said. "According to that pastor in Rott's hometown, Rott's got a rich relative down here somewhere. Could be it's Casper Leavitt. Remember what I told you about that note in Faust's file cabinet? 'Funds for Fun in the Sun?' The call I made to that number? Makes sense, I think. Leavitt and Rott."

Diane said, "They had Faust point the finger at Moses after Ferdie died. No wonder Faust didn't want to talk. Weiler's a nasty guy to have in the other corner."

"So's Casper, from everything I've heard."

"What about that Miami thing, though?"

"I know. Rott couldn't have done the killing. Miami's how far from Orlando? Half a day's drive?"

Diane leaned back, closed her eyes like she felt the hour. "I guess Ferdie really could've committed suicide. They made things bad enough for him."

Gun was silent. His eyes stung with the lateness. He had the dreamlike sensation that his eyes and ears were fuzzing out from too much concentration and coffee. He'd thought, when they began, that the tapes and the notes would make everything clear, including

Moses: that they'd learn, like Billy, why Ferdie was murdered, and by whom. He'd been certain it was Rott Weiler until Harold Ibbins came on the tape and confounded it all—Rott had reasons to kill Ferdie, probably would've liked to, but he wasn't even there. Now everything was scattering. Harold and Miss Mary entered Gun's mind the way he'd seen them last, and Billy Apple, and Neil Faust in the ice wash.

Diane said, "I have to sleep."

Something was down there, down in the whirling. Some tiny rock-hard conviction that told him there was happy news in all this, only it wasn't getting to the part of his brain that told him things. He closed his eyes, kept them still so the sand in them wouldn't scrape. The conviction grew.

She stood. "You can have the stateroom. Bed's almost long enough for you."

"Wait."

It wouldn't go away. Too much information and something in it didn't fit. Gun pressed the bridge of his nose and thought, *Come to me*.

And it came, fighting him, like a recalcitrant puppy.

"Well, what do you know?" he muttered.

"Not enough," she said.

"There is a bitter little man in a wheelchair," he told her, "who collects the signatures of ballplayers. On March seventh, 1977, he collected Rott's. In Orlando. In the evening."

She squinted in the old light.

"Rott," he said, "was supposed to be in Miami with a giggling girlfriend. Remember? Wasn't going to open the shades for a whole day. Except on the same day, he got nailed by this old guy in the wheelchair. In a lowlife bar."

"He lied to Ibbins?"

"It would appear."

"He wanted Ibbins to think he was out of town—"

"He wanted *everyone* to think he was out of town,"

Gun said, "if anyone ever asked. But they never did."
He got to his feet. "He was so effective getting
everyone to look at Moses, nobody questioned Rott.
He had an escape hatch, and he never had to use it."

She stared at him with her cheeks coloring like two
maple leaves, and knowing what he knew shook the
tiredness from him like water. His eyes were clear and
hers were clear and shiny with adrenaline, and it was a
good thing because the boat yawed suddenly with
footsteps on the deck overhead and the hatch
slammed open sounding hollow. Gun shoved Diane
into the narrow head and grabbed a paring knife out
of the sink. Somebody dropped through the hatch and
landed without grace on the teak flooring.

"Man, you doing!" said Clarence Coldspring. He
stood and weaved, smelling of beer and a hundred
unfiltered Camels. Diane stepped out from the head
and Clarence grinned at Gun.

"I thought you'd be here, big man," he said.

Diane said, "Clarence—"

"Glad of it, too," Clarence said. "We could use you.
My little brother, he was over at Leavitt's tonight.
Stealin' fowl. He heard 'em gettin' ready, Casper's
boys. Sayin' it's time to visit the Coldsprings. This
time, hey, we're gonna be ready."

33

There was a coil of heavy wire in the back of Clarence's decayed Land Rover that skidded wheelwell-to-
wheelwell every time they hit a hole. There were lots
of holes. Lots of wire up front, too, holding door

handles on, the glove box shut, the rearview in place. Clarence applied alternately too much gas and too much clutch, shouting, "Ho, man! Ho, man!" as the Rover yipped and scratched over pitted black-top.

A few miles west of Indiantown they turned north on a lumpy two-tracked field road that showed salt white in the headlights. Clarence stopped his yelling and went grim as he drove, leaning forward over the wheel. Gun could see the remains of rotted fence posts rising out of the land then bumping past on his right. Hanging rags on sprung barbed wire. A gate. Clarence cut the lights and motor and the Land Rover thumped to a halt.

Engineless they could hear crickets, the distant metronomic bark of a dog, the cicada waltz around them in the swelling dark. The air smelled of oranges, a ways off.

"No noise," Clarence said. "We beat 'em here. Or else," he added, "they been here already."

"Where are we?" Gun couldn't see any houses.

Clarence went to the Rover and undid the wire that held the back shut. He reached in and withdrew a long high-beam flashlight that looked worth more than the vehicle. He stripped off his black T-shirt and stretched it across the lens and snapped the light on. It still threw a good beam across the field but the small round brilliance of lens and bulb was clouded over. He pointed with the light.

"We go over the little rise. A dozen shacks in a row. We go in careful so the old man don't shoot us thinkin' it's Casper, and we wait." Clarence rubbed his narrow chest, quietly murdered a mosquito. "Know what?" he said. "Guns are something we don't got much of." He went back to the Rover and got the coil of wire. He got a good grip and yanked it into an oval, then twisted it tight until it made a heavy, flexible two-foot club several inches thick.

"You smack a guy with that," he said, handing it

over, "he's gonna know it, but not until a whole lot later."

They went slowly up the rise with the light trained low ahead of them, reached the top. Kneeling there they could make out a long narrow shed with a slanted roof opposite the small gray humps of Coldspring shacks. The windows were black. A limber gray shadow separated itself from one of the shacks and prowled forward.

"That's Early," Clarence whispered. "Got us on the wind."

Early was the mostly blue tick hunting hound that had so proudly reunited the Coldsprings with their departed kin. She glided up the grassy hill toward them, smelling Clarence, hind end wagging. Clarence laughed softly. The earth was cool and sweet under their knees. Reaching them the dog sniffed Gun's hand, approved, and butted Clarence in the chest with its nose.

"Playtime you think, hey?" Clarence whispered. Early whined yes. Clarence, holding the light, did the habitual thing. He chuckled, rubbed the dog's head, and stood up against the sky.

34

The small-caliber bullet that finally nestled at the tip of Clarence's collarbone would've gone a lot worse except that it took Early first. The big hound was up on its hind legs embracing Clarence when Gun saw a round hole open on its white hide and a moment later heard the shot. Early was dead almost before the slug was out of her body, the hollow point coming out tired and plocking itself into Clarence, quitting in the soft place barely under the skin.

They landed in the grass with Early on top and Clarence rolled the dog off in a sort of one-shouldered panic. "Pricks, pricks, sonsabitches—" he squealed until Gun stifled him with a palm and held him still. The flashlight was still on, smothered under Early. There'd been just the one shot, nothing more, but now looking at the row of shacks Gun saw gray doors cracking open to black. In at least one of the doors he detected the chill oiled glow of gunmetal, and for the moment it took to register the smells of sweat and cooling dust, Gun thought Clarence had been shot by his own family. Then he saw someone, a small boy from his ducking swiftness, slip out of one of the shacks and start for them, and another shot ruined the quiet and then two more. Slaps of light showed like heat lightning from behind the long shed and the boy disappeared around one of the shacks.

Clarence was twisting. Gun became aware of pain in his hand and discovered that Clarence was biting him, hard, in the thickness below the thumb. He jerked free.

"Lemme up, man," Clarence hissed, gasping. "I ain't no woman. Where are they?"

"The shed."

"Chickenshit." Clarence was squeezing his right shoulder with his left hand, rotating it. There were tears on his face.

"Let me see."

Clarence shook his head. "Hardly any blood even. I could get the damn thing out with my teeth if I wanted to. What we do is—" but more gunfire wrecked his instructions, the deep bellow of a large-bore shotgun, two shots piling up on each other and making concussions in the earth.

"Gordon's double-barrel," said Clarence. "Oughta knock that shed right down."

Gun had a look. Seeing was all but impossible but it seemed that two shapes, large ones bent at the waist, were running from the shed. A third left the shadow of the nearest shack and darted after the boy who'd drawn fire. Gun said, "Stay here," and went for them fast, his feet uncertain in the dark as if the ground itself were newly made. The movement shook what little vision he had and he lost the men, saw them again as a lamp came on in one of the windows and they ran past it, the light putting yellow stains on their dark hooded windbreakers. Inside someone shouted, Gun almost close enough now to make words of it, his feet getting confidence and hitting easy, and nearing the light he reached back hoping he still had the big lungs and sprinted down the row of shacks. Gaining on the windbreakers he passed the window and there were again shouts behind it and immediately an enormous blast of powder and pane that made the air around him shine with shivered glass like a winter's worth of frost. There was a feeling like frost, too, at the back of his neck, like ice there and still running he felt with his fingers. Slickness. His feet were back to clumsy and sounded muffled and he realized his ears were gone from the explosion. He hoped they'd return and ran on, forgetting who he was chasing. The windbreakers. They'd been up ahead but weren't now and Gun was out of shacks, out of legs, out of ears. He slowed, stopped, sat down on prairie grass to breathe. Such dark, such quiet, too, except inside the skull where the pounding noises were. Like gravel. He closed his eyes and listened: like a duffel bag of gravel bumping down a set of metal stairs.

He waited while his wind came back and then reached to his neck again, blood-shiny with the little glass gnats from the shack window. The blood made him remember Clarence, back there with Early on top of the hill.

In his head the duffel bumped down a few more stairs, only now it was Clarence in the bag instead of gravel and he was making noises.

Mmiigg maannn.

Yup, that'd be him.

The pounding subsided at last to where Gun could feel the steadiness of the cicada hum moving through him without interruption and he took this as a sign that he would hear again.

Aaay miig mannn.

The duffel bag was about gone but Clarence was getting clearer. It came to Gun through a layer of numb that perhaps the noise was now coming from outside his head, and he opened his eyes and turned.

It wasn't Clarence, although the voice even distorted carried the same high tension. This boy was crouching a few yards behind him in a stance that displayed both caution and deftness. Gun risked starting the duffel again and spoke.

"You the little brother? Clarence's?"

"Big brother," said the kid, the *b*s resonating like he was talking into a snare drum.

"Is everyone all right?"

"We got Clarence." Gun heard some smile in the voice. "You all right, big man?"

They had him in the shack next to the one with the blown-out window. The floor was whitewashed pine boards laid loose over bare dirt. Electricity came in through a thick black cord hanging down from the ceiling; it hooked up to one bare bulb, sixty watt, a brown Warm Morning space heater in the middle of the room, and a color console television so old the screen had rounded corners. The TV was on, Angie Dickinson as Police Woman looking dated but pretty good, and Clarence was watching on the couch. His shirt was off and the hole was cleaned up already and patched with white paste and cotton.

"Looka here," he said, holding up a clear glass jar. It held a bit of mushroomed lead. "Bullet. Gram took it out. See," he said, nodding at the TV, "Angie's got nothin' on me."

"Wrong, boy," said a little wrinkled man in a rocker next to the couch. He had gray braids that went to his waist. "Angie got everything on you."

"Ha, gramp."

Gram Coldspring, twice her husband's size, her hair still black, ramrodded into the room carrying coffee. She poked a mug at Gun, dropping her eyes.

"Gram, he's bleedin'," Clarence said.

It took Gram five minutes with a hot cloth and tweezers to get the visible chunks of window out of Gun's neck. The pain set his mind upright again and he started wondering about earlier. Clarence's brother —big brother?—was sitting cross-legged next to the couch, looking at Clarence with concern and ordering Gram to produce more coffee.

"How'd they manage to miss you?" Gun asked him. "When you came out and started for us, after they hit

Clarence . . . one of them was right on your back-side."

The brother stared at him without comprehension. "*Who* came out?" Clarence demanded.

"No way was it me," said the brother. "I hear that first shot, I'm stickin' my head in the pillow."

"Christian, musta been," Clarence said, and to Gun, "my little brother. The one heard Leavitt's guys, earlier."

The old man came with effort out of the rocker and turned off Angie, who was snuggling a dope dealer. "Gram!" he shouted. "You find Christian!"

And Gram looked, and then with the sweat beginning to move again so did everyone else, but there was no Christian Coldspring.

35

What they had to do at last was go outside and spread out like bush-beaters after prey. Dawn was coming with a dusty bloom in the east that seemed to chill what remained of the night. A dozen Coldsprings holding guns and hoes fanned out north and east, away from the highway. Only Gram stayed behind.

Casper Leavitt's property ran mostly to pasture and swamp, with a few hundred acres of orange trees on the north end where Casper lived. He was reputed to favor the smell of citrus over that of cows and Coldsprings, and he had enough land to make his

world essentially what he wanted. Gun figured him for
a sort he'd run across before—men whose personali-
ties pushed them uphill until they stood at the top of
their unhappy fiefdoms, consuming their women and
directing their serfs from afar. It was the Steinbren-
ner effect Gun had seen in baseball and sometimes
elsewhere. Fifty yards to his right Gramp Coldspring saluted Gun with his weapon of choice, a
splintered axe handle. It was time to march with the
serfs.

The attackers had taken Christian and fled on foot,
at least for a distance; no one had heard them arrive,
and afterward there'd been no giveaway sounds of
ignition. Because of this and because the bodies of
Clarence's great-uncle and cousin had been found in
Casper's boggy bottomland, Gun found himself part
of a wide scythe-shaped line sweeping out toward the
quiet swamp. He had the improvised wire club from
Clarence. It seemed to him a far crusade from what
he'd expected when Jack first caught him in the fish
house and told him about the message from Moses
Gates.

The pasture had been cowless long enough to make
walking easy and with daybreak near the line moved
quickly, heads down scanning the tall grass. Gun
began to see that the Coldsprings already half expected Christian to be dead, to find him there blud-
geoned on Casper's ground. He heard a long-ago
sound on the morning breeze and it was Gramp
singing slowly as if in mourning. The grass as he
moved through it had a fresh yellow smell that went
sour as they came closer to the swamp. The singing got
fainter and Gun realized the line was spreading apart.
There was a low rise in the land and then the swamp
lay before them, green and woven, and beyond it the
uniform rows of trees, branches bent low with fruit.
The sun inched up now and with its first ray lit up a

rectangle at the crest of the grove. Gun squinted. A window. A high gable on a distant house.

By the time they reached the swamp they were a hundred yards apart. Gun saw Gramp reach the rushes and step in without faltering. He disappeared as if into a cornfield. Gun did likewise and suddenly there was no sky, only the green scratchiness of bullrush above and around him and underneath an earth that sagged with his weight. He stepped forward and the rushes zipped closed behind him. They filled his stinging ears with whispers. He wondered at their chances of finding Christian here and wished the dog Early was alive and plunging along beside them. He took more steps, trying to keep them straight, remembering the time he'd heard a Catholic talking earnestly about Purgatory and realizing that this was it, cut off from sunlight with dread fear just a thin crust away, and thinking this he heard the low groan of a sinner.

He stopped his feet and listened.

The groan again, punctuated by hog grunts. It wasn't Purgatory anymore. The rushes whispered urgently but anguish and bestial glee came through like a sound burped up from Hell. It was close on Gun's right and he swung the wire club like a machete, breaking through. The groans faded under his own thrashing until he was right on them in a little matted clearing where the sky showed again. Christian was gagged and on his gut, shirtless. Two guys were with him, a tall one in a windbreaker and a fat football-coach type in rubber boots holding a three-foot piece of steel. Windbreaker had a rifle and that was worse—a club you could dodge. Gun dove for him as the barrel came up and sent everything he could through the twisted wire and into Windbreaker's right ankle. It brought a scream that sounded all wrong amidst the rushes and the guy dropped next to Christian while the football coach squatted and maneuvered for position. Windbreaker still had the rifle and with one hand tried to point it but Gun on one knee gripped the stock and twisted, catching the man's finger in the trigger guard and popping it free of the joint. For the length of another scream he had the gun to himself, and then fire rippled through him from behind and his muscles got stupid and he dropped the rifle and fell on his side in the weeds. Grabbing the gun the fat man tossed it gently to the edge of the tiny clearing. He stood over Gun who sat up slowly trying to unmuck his brain.

"It's a hell of a surprise, isn't it?" said the football coach, waving his piece of steel which Gun now saw was a cattle prod. "Volts, amps, I don't know. Don't pay no attention. What I know is, ain't a steer I ever worked with didn't live in mortal dread of this thing." With a fleetness that belied his size the fat man thrust the prod at Gun. He parried with a forearm and the roll of electricity sucked his breath from him, peeled back his nerves like a sleeve. He felt the swamp crust shake when his head hit it and lying there he smelled burned skin. Beside him the tall man panted swear words into his ruined hand. Christian Coldspring's eyes over the gag were narrow and hopeless. Gun flexed the muscles in his arms and they told him no thanks, they'd just done a thousand push-ups.

"The hell're you doin' here anyhow, big fella?" said the football coach. "Got some kinda Indian love-in goin' on? You look about as Coldspring as—hell, as *I* do!" His voice was frustrated, as if he'd just noticed for the first time he'd been zapping a white guy.

The wire club lay to Gun's left where it had fallen, all but two inches of it hidden in the standing rushes. Five feet distant. Maybe six.

"Ought to have stayed outa the swamp, anyhow," Coach went on. "Most of the time it's safe, ya know, it stays asleep. But every now and again," he winked at Christian and lowered his voice to a whisper, "it wakes up, and *eats* folks." He started to reach for the rifle but there was a sudden extra rustle in the weeds and he paused to peer into them. Gun did a roll that felt like the bad slow-motion in scary dreams and caught the wire club just as Coach was thundering down with the prod again. He rolled back and the fat man missed, vanished for a moment in the rushes. Panicked at this Windbreaker made a pathetic swipe at Gun with his good hand but Gun swung the club backhanded, laid the guy cold across Christian Coldspring's knees. Coach came struggling back before Gun could reach the rifle and feinted desperately with the prod. The rushes grew louder around them. Coach's eyes were red and nervous and he made the adrenal farmyard grunts Gun had heard over Christian's groans. At last he pulled the prod back like a switch and aimed a stroke at Gun's midsection that came in whistling. There was only one way to react and Gun regretted it even as he swung his club to block the big prod. The club was steel wire and in addition to being heavy and effective was the finest conductor of electricity he could've chosen. His hands went white and frozen as the blast traveled into them and his mind turned to TV snow, understanding only that try as he might he could not let the damn club loose. It clung to the prod like a magnet, his muscles wearing down while Coach sweated in his rubber boots and kept the pressure on, and it was only after the static in the brain seemed to seep out and make sparks in the open air that he heard a brief *thack* and his eyes made sense again and he went panting to his knees.

"Ah," said Gramp Coldspring. He was sweating too and had his braids thrown back over his shoulders. He looked about as happy as Gun imagined he could look. He had a cleanup hitter's grip on the splintered axe handle, and there was a little of Coach's scalp up on the sweet spot.

"Ah," he said again, greatly satisfied.

Coach was on his face, limp as a 250-pound rat.

Christian was hugging his grandfather's knees.

Gun said, "Thank you. Thank you, very much."

36

"Home," said Gramp, lifting Christian into the air.

Gun nodded down at Coach and said, "Go ahead, Gramp, I think I'll try to bring this big one around, make sure he's not dead or anything." If the guy was breathing, you couldn't tell it. No sounds of pain, no movement between the shoulder blades, nothing.

"Don't bother. They'll bury him themselves." Gramp spit next to Coach's body and swung Christian up onto his back and headed out of the swamp the way he'd come in.

"I'll be with you in a minute," Gun said, and knelt down to feel for a pulse in Coach's neck. He found it right away, a strong one, too. He turned the man over and slapped his muddy face, heard a small groan. "Okay, time to wake up and talk," he said.

It was an old trick his father had taught him, an army trick from basic training, wake a guy up every time, no matter how tired or drunk or sick. What you did was grip the sleeper's thumb between your index finger and your own thumb, and press down hard with your thumbnail on the guy's cuticle. "Bring him out of a coma, if that's what you need," Gun's father liked to say. And it worked on Coach just fine. Gun squeezed extra hard and Coach sat up like he had springs in his back, swearing fast and well. Then he was holding his head between his elbows and crying tears.

Gun told him to shut up for a minute and Coach bit his lip, jaw still going. "You're going to take me to see Casper now," Gun said. "He and I've got some things to discuss. Important things. Where's he at?"

Coach seemed to have lost his language facility, needed help getting to his feet and putting one in front of the other, but in fifteen minutes they'd left the swamp behind and were walking through a lovely orchard of ripening oranges, row after row of heavy-limbed trees. Gun was beginning to wonder, though, if maybe Coach was leading him the wrong way when they suddenly stepped out from the orchard into a clearing. Fifty yards off, in the center of a perfect lawn, was the house, a square, three-storey brick colonial.

"This here is Casper's," said Coach, with reverence.

"You can still talk, I'm glad of it," Gun said.

"Casper'd be out in the garage. Where he spends his time mostly."

"I don't see it."

"Around back," said Coach.

Gun expected something different than he got. The garage didn't match the house or even come close. It was a small wood-frame structure that would have fit with a middle-class rambler. Two doors in the front, windowless, a four-sided roof that came to a point at the top where a little tin chimney stuck out. The building badly needed paint and one door had been punched in by a bumper. As they neared it, Gun heard the sound of country music coming from inside. Coach knocked on the door.

"Who's the shithead?" The voice was rough and high.

"Edwood," Coach answered. He sounded scared, and glanced over at Gun for direction.

"Tell him you got *me* here, Gun Pedersen."

Coach took a breath and looked straight up—for courage? Moving his shoulders around. Where the piece of scalp was gone from his head there was a raw wound the size of a half-dollar. "I got a guy here by the name of Gun Pedersen that says he wants to see you, Mr. Leavitt. Sorry."

"Then bring him in here—goddamnit, Edwood— where he *can* see me."

Coach opened the door and stepped out of the way for Gun to enter first, which he did, looking around for the man and finding him on a broken-down sofa in the middle of more garbage than Gun had seen since helping Ruben Caulich, Stony's junkman, look for a used gas tank for the old Ford. Old televisions and tube radios, rusty bicycles, stacks of molding *Playboys* and *National Geographics* and *Reader's Digests*, all sorts of clocks, cheap plastic stereo components, record albums without covers, wrecked power tools, old hand tools, lawn furniture made from nylon plumbing pipe. All of it the kind of stuff you could buy for a buck or two at a garage sale, and candy wrappers, too, Salted Nut Roll and Moon Pies mostly, wadded up and strewn everywhere, and empty bottles of Dixie Beer, lots of them.

Looking perfectly comfortable in the midst of this disorder was a fat man with deep-set eyes that looked even deeper because of the heavy thicket of gray brow exploding above them. His features were distorted by excess flesh and he wore bib overalls with no shirt underneath and a pair of rubber thongs that displayed his yellowed toenails. To Gun, though, the most surprising thing about his appearance was his nose. Remarkably well-formed, long and narrow with artic- ulated nostrils, it didn't belong in this face, in this garage, but rather on someone with a body and a sense of beauty to do it justice. Probably looked all right, Gun thought, in Leavitt's soap-opera house.

"Casper Leavitt," the man said. "Pleased to know you, Pedersen. Edwood, you can take your ass out of here, thank you very much." Leavitt pointed to a chair next to a small humming refrigerator, leaned over and flicked the OFF button on a boom-box.

"Doesn't seem right, you in here looking so comfortable, and your boys out molesting kids," Gun said.

Apparently Leavitt thought this was funny because he laughed, or tried to. It was more like a cough with a smile behind it. "Them Coldsprings are *all* children, Pedersen, you gotta understand. And like children they need the rod once in a while, otherwise they get outa hand. You got kids, right? Oof, Indians, they got no respect for property. Live on my land like it's their own private reservation and take my fowl with impunity. I can't let it happen, can't let 'em walk over me when*ever* they please. I gotta stand up for myself *once* in a while. Oof, shit."

"And every so often you're obligated to go out and kill one to teach the rest a lesson. Is that about right?"

"You been kissin' the wrong asses, baseball man. You do that and you hear the wrong side of the story—or just one side. Ask them Indians about killing, they can tell you some stuff. I won't deny their blood's been spilled some, too, like ours, but we're not talking murder. Oof. Anybody turns up dead and it's a war casualty. Different ethics at work there, ask anybody with a college degree. Course, human life is human life and precious, and all that happy horseshit, and I regret the tragedies. But the fact is, them people can leave any day they want. Pack up and go. I'm not saying stay. Hey, reach into that icebox there, and grab me a coupla them Moon Pies. Have one yourself."

"No thanks." Gun opened the fridge and tossed

Leavitt the candy he wanted, watched the man peel away the wrappers from both before he began to eat the first one.

"But let's be honest, here. Reason you want to see me isn't the Indians. Oh, you love them, too, but it's that black friend of yours, Gates, right? You want to know what the dead reporter was scratching away at here. Besides little brown assholes."

"I want to know about Rott Weiler, too," Gun said. "And Neil Faust."

"Oof, Robert." Leavitt shut his eyes and paused for a moment in his chewing. "And Neil's a piss-ant."

"Are we going to talk?" Gun asked.

"Course we are." Leavitt's eyes snapped open, his eyebrows shook. "I don't have nothing to hide. But we got to back up a little, slow down, let you hear the whole thing, not just part, you know what I mean? People're always settling for part and it makes me goddamned upset. Oof, shit." He pointed at the refrigerator again, his tongue going over his lips, and Gun tossed him two more Moon Pies.

"First I gotta establish something, bottom line. You're sittin' here, already thinking it comes down to the almighty buck and that's not how it is. No, it's principles we'll be talkin' about now. I've got 'em and you've got 'em, and they're sure as hell not the same, yours and mine, but that's okay. I happen to believe in the separation of the races, not the killing off of people, understand, but the *integrity* of bloodlines. Now I don't give a shit what you think. I'm tellin' you what I think. And the red people and the black people and them there Jews and Italians, and all that, I say they have every right to live and be happy and shit, but they can go do it some other goddamn place. That's what I believe, and have ever since I was just a little bastard. And sometimes it's not easy, having convictions that're unpopular. Hasn't been for me, I'll tell you. But I stuck by my principles, and it paid off. Paid off real good." Leavitt took a half a Moon Pie in his mouth, chewed twice, and smiled. "Here's how it went for me. Now listen up."

The fat man had been sliding lower in the sofa and now, with effort, he moved himself so he was lying down, head propped on one armrest, his hands folded over the top of his belly like a man in a casket. He kept one eye on Gun as he talked, a hyperalert eye that recorded every reaction then reacted itself: widening, narrowing down, rarely blinking. "I'm a poor kid from Missoura, right, and I come down to the hot state to find my fortune. Actually I'm in the service, navy, and I'm stationed at Cape Canaveral, and I meet this old gentleman at a nice little whitesonly gathering one night, and we hit it off good. He's crippled up and needing help and I'm the guy that offers. This is just about the time I get my honorable discharge and I didn't know shit about him 'cepting that he and I, we see the world the same way and he needs somebody younger than himself to take care of stuff he can't. He's got this orange farm and wants a guy to drive him around, put some of the help in their place once in a while, shit like that. And I'm his guy.

"This goes on for a year and when he dies I find myself holding the bag, and buddy, it's gold. He's got kids but they're liberals now, bleeding all over themselves, don't ask me how, and he gives it all to me, right down to the nickel. The orange farm and his stash and hell, every little piece of this world he can't take with him. I am *truly* set up, and it's a fairy tale, and I'm grateful, too. And I tell you all this because later, when my nephew Robert comes by needing help—and I see that he's got hold of the same principles I do—well, it's not easy for me to say no. It goes pretty hard on my conscience, being I've got it in my power to make his life one hell of a lot better, just like old Henry'd done for me." Leavitt turned full toward Gun and scowled, his eyebrows gathering like thunderheads on his forehead. "You *did* know Robert was my nephew, yes?"

"I thought so," Gun said. "But what did he want from you, exactly?"

"Oof, shit, it wasn't so wise of me, looking back. But he had good reasons, and now I keep telling myself this. You know of course that Robert was playing ball then, the Minnesota club, and not playing well at all. Very depressed. And he's like a son to me, you gotta understand. We think the same about the really important things. Goddamn it, he knows where the real threat comes from, not the communists— hell, they're all eating hamburgers now and crapping in pay toilets, tell me about *them*. No, it's a genetic holocaust we're headed for. The destruction of the one race in history that managed to bring mankind out of the jungle and into civilization." Leavitt swept his arm through the air and Gun took another look around the man's garage. "Rott understands this and it makes me sympathetic. What he wanted was help disgracing an idiot that fully deserved it. A guy that promoted racial integration and not only that, was disloyal to his teammates." Leavitt sighed and relaxed again on the couch.

Gun said, "Ferdie and Rott also happened to want the same job, don't forget that."

"I know. That made it more complicated, I should have thought about it more. I also didn't mean for it to end like it did. Honestly didn't have any killing in mind." Leavitt's eye narrowed at Gun. "You knew about that, too, of course."

Gun nodded. "But what did *you* do?" he asked.

"Me? Robert wasn't into the big contract yet, so I gave him the cash he needed in order to make life better for Faust. That's all I did. Then Robert got carried away, scared Millevich'd get the thing figured out. Panicked like the dumbass he is."

"What about Billy, though? And Ibbins?"

"Oof, shit. I don't know. You gotta ask Rott about them. I've got nothing to do with it. Rott's on his own now."

"Just a minute," Gun said. "I don't think he is. You just told me yourself that Billy wasn't out here only for the sake of the Coldsprings. Finish your story."

"I'm finished with my story. Billy was out here because he learned I was Robert's uncle, and figured that little fact would lead to more. He was wrong. What killed him, I suppose, was trying to get Faust to talk, which got back to Robert who must've panicked again. But that's only theory. Like I said, Robert's on his own now. I don't know diddly about this latest mess of his."

"That's it?" Gun asked. "You don't seem to care a whole lot what happens to your nephew. Or to you, for that matter."

"Nothing's gonna happen to me. All I did was give a kid some money a long time ago. They don't arrest a guy for that, even if he *is* a goddamn bigot. Now Robert, he might try to pass the guilt around, the boy's got no loyalty. But that's fine. He won't be able to put a thing on me. You watch."

"I will," Gun said, standing. "First, though, I'm going to have a talk with your nephew. There's going to be a lot of people wanting to talk with your nephew."

"Be my guest, all of you." Leavitt sat up halfway on the couch and motioned for Gun to throw him more candy.

"You need the exercise," Gun said. He walked toward the door, pushed it open and looked back once more at Leavitt.

The man sighed loudly and shook his large head. "Edwood!" he called.

37

Gun waited until late morning to visit Rott, too late as it turned out. He figured there was no hurry now, and he needed the sleep after all, but when he arrived at the farm at a quarter to twelve the man wasn't home, and he had to settle instead for Louis, who was out in the front yard using rope to stake down newly planted palm trees against the threat of wind.

"Where do you think he's at?" Gun asked. "They're not playing till tonight, are they?"

Louis tied off a knot expertly and slashed away the extra length of rope with a small razor knife. "Think he went to the park early. Some of them guys can't hit as good as they should. Them guys need more batting practice."

"You're handy with that rope, Louis," Gun said, watching him tie another knot.

Louis looked up then and Gun saw pride, and something else, too, in his eyes. "Rott, he counts on me," Louis said.

Gun didn't find Rott at the ballpark, not on the field and not in the locker room. But leaving the clubhouse he found someone else.

Jacobson Cleary was, as usual, blocking the way with his chair. Today he wore a tie with a photograph of himself silk-screened onto it. The image of his head was elongated, making him resemble a grasshopper, the dark-rimmed glasses a pair of insect eyes.

"Roll," Gun said. "I'm in a hurry."

"And why might that be?" Jacobson Cleary withdrew his hand, empty, from beneath the seat and placed it courteously in his skinny lap.

"I'm looking for Rott. You know where he is?"

"Rott—yes, of course. Ah, that's wonderful. You figured it out, I can see it in your face. Robert Weiler." Cleary rubbed his palms together fast enough to create heat.

"Do you know where he is?"

"I do." The old man leaned his narrow head against the backrest of his chair and sighted down through the black-framed glasses resting on the tip of his nose. "Please, I'm dreadfully curious—tell me everything at once."

"Later." Gun stepped around the chair and, as he did, Jacobson Cleary opened his mouth impossibly wide—it looked like a cavern appearing out of nowhere—and let out a delighted laugh.

"Please, not so quick, Mr. Pedersen. You tell me and I'll tell you. Fair enough? You *do* want Weiler, don't you? Today?"

Gun's hands wanted to wring the old man's frail neck, but they had to settle for being jammed into pockets.

"You wouldn't lay a hand on me," said Cleary. "You're too civilized for your own good." He smiled up at Gun, his face wide open, expectant, full of pure happiness. "So, what was it? The card I got from Rott the night Ferdie kicked off?"

"That was a good part of it," said Gun. "How'd you know?"

"No, you go first. Then me. What made it click for you? Come on, man. Tell me about it, I've been waiting ten years." Leaning forward, licking his lips, blinking, Cleary was all attention, the devil at a deathbed.

"Billy Apple's interview tape with Ibbins," said Gun. "Seems Ibbins got a phone call that night from Rott, early evening, probably not long before you got him to put his Hancock on the card. Thing is, Rott claimed to be down in Miami with a girlfriend. Rott was just trying to build himself an alibi."

"Ah," said Cleary, shaking his head. "You see, that's the piece I was missing. I didn't know about the call to Harold."

"I don't get why the card meant anything at all to you," said Gun. "Rott never had to *use* the alibi."

"No, he didn't have to use it. But at the time, he didn't *know* he wouldn't have to use it. So what did he do? He tried to get the card back. Listen. Next day, who should show up at my place but that dim-witted Louis character, wanting back the card I'd signed for Rott. I had the presence of mind to tell him I'd already gotten rid of it. Sold it to the College of Baseball Knowledge, I told him. A little shop they had on the west side of town. Cards, memorabilia. And of course Louis believed me." Cleary paused, then added quietly, "That night the place burned to the ground." The old man lifted both hands to his face and for an instant Gun saw flames in his eyes. "I never knew exactly how that card fit the puzzle, but I knew Rott was behind it. I knew it."

"And you didn't do a thing," Gun said.

Cleary closed his eyes and nodded. For a few moments his face seemed to register remorse, but then his eyes snapped open again and the glint was back in them. "I am a very intelligent man, Mr. Pedersen, and I don't say that boastfully. It's a fact. Intelligence and courage, however, are two very distinct and different qualities. *But,* the truth is I did do something. Not for a long time, true, but if you think I wasn't taking my miserable life into my hands, walking into the bar like I did last week and showing off that card to you boys, you're very mistaken. Bravest thing I've ever done. Now, I advise you to go directly to a dismal little place called Rory's on the Water. You know it, I'm sure, right next to the drawbridge on the Intracoastal. This side. The older ballplayers love it there. Seems to attract the groupies who are past their better days."

Gun, already heading for his rented car, shouted thanks over his shoulder.

"You're welcome, sir," said Jacobson Cleary.

Rory's was just a couple miles away and Gun hit mostly green lights and made it in less than five minutes. The building was rounded at both ends and fashioned to resemble a tugboat. It sat almost directly beneath a drawbridge spanning the intracoastal waterway between mainland Florida and the long strip of offshore island where the money showed. Gun went inside and found Rott sitting in a booth with a pair of men Gun recognized as coaches for the Toucans.

"Hey, Gun Pedersen, whatch you all doin' here?" Rott was at his southern best, beer-happy and welcoming. "Sit down and join the party. Slide over, Harry, and make room."

Gun sat down and let himself be introduced to the two men and given a draft beer. He sat for fifteen, twenty minutes listening to baseball talk. Tonight was the first game of the last series between Tallahassee and West Palm, and Tallahassee had a two-game edge. Rott was confident and loud, sure of a Senior-League championship saying, The big's need me. His coaches mostly listened, wagging their heads and making agreeable noises. Gun excused himself and went to make a couple phone calls. One to Sergeant Morrell of the West Palm Police Department. One to Diane Apple.

When he came back, he told Rott they needed to talk.

"Shit, Gun, you look pretty serious. What's the deal?" Rott swallowed the last of his current beer and pulled back a little from the table, blinking.

"It's about Moses, sort of. Something you need to know about. Let's take a little walk." Gun nodded out the window, where he saw the drawbridge lifting and a long white yacht with a high mast approaching from the north.

"Well, hell. Okay. Moses, you say?"

Gun and Rott left Rory's and walked up the steep sidewalk toward the street fronting the Intracoastal, then toward the bridge, which was fully raised now. The yacht was still a hundred yards north.

"Let's hear it," Rott said, glancing over at Gun. His milky blue eyes were red from the beer, and he licked his lips nervously.

"Like I said, it's only sort of about Moses. It's also about you," Gun said. "And about Ferdie. And Billy, and Ibbins and Neil Faust."

"What the hell kind of a thing to say is that?"

Gun stopped at the edge of the bridge, thinking, Let's not put this off any longer. "Rott, listen."

"I'm listening, and you better watch what you say, old buddy, 'cause it sounds pretty goddamn careless to me."

"I had a long talk last night with your uncle," Gun said. "I learned quite a bit, too."

"My uncle?"

"Casper Leavitt."

Rott's eyes cleared a little and he straightened up, tucked his shirt into his pants, and pulled his belly in. "Say it," he said.

"Leavitt told me about you and Neil Faust, the arrangement you two had. He also doesn't think Ferdie Millevich killed himself. He thinks you killed Ferdie."

"He's a goddamned liar, then." Rott looked over his shoulder, then ahead. The yacht had passed through now, and the long halves of the bridge were beginning to come down, slowly. "That's bullshit."

"Maybe," Gun said. "Your uncle might not be a fellow you can put your trust in. But there's something else, too. I heard some tapes of Billy Apple's. He had them hidden in his boat."

"Boat?" Rott said quickly.

"Bet you didn't know he had one. But he did, and that's where he kept his notes and tapes, everything he knew about you and Faust and everybody else. He talked to your old friend Ibbins, too, and wouldn't you know, Ibbins remembered that little story you gave him about staying with some girlfriend in Miami, same night Ferdie died. Same night you gave Cleary your John Hancock in Orlando. And then it hit me. A guy can't be in two places at one time. Just isn't possible."

He felt Rott tense, almost sensed the ripple going through his legs like they were getting ready to spring. Gun put a hand on his shoulder. "Don't think about going anyplace. It's too late for that."

Rott's eyes were sharper than Gun had ever seen them, the milkiness gone completely. "It's not true, Gun, you gotta believe me."

A police car swung into view, two blocks north, and came toward them. No speed, no sirens.

Gun said, "You can tell your side of it to all the right people now, Rott. If I've got it wrong, set me straight."

The police car came on and now a second one appeared, from the south. Rott looked from one car to the other. He seemed to momentarily shut down, then suddenly awoke, threw a fist into Gun's midsection, and ran past the lineup of waiting cars and straight up the middle of the descending bridge. The incline was about thirty degrees and dropping, and he ran in a crouch, fast, almost on all fours, like a lanky, poorly coordinated dog. Gun chased after him, feeling the angle of rise shifting beneath, the work becoming easier as the bridge fell to horizontal. He caught up with Rott at the end of the half section of bridge, put a hand on the waistband of Rott's pants and pulled him back. Rott spun around, swinging, and Gun felt the impact on his temple, the rough hot surface of concrete on the palms of his hands. He shook his head to bring sight back into his eyes and looked up in time to see Rott leap from the end of the section, arms reaching for the end of the other half, which was ten feet away now and closing fast.

Rott's jump was too short.

His feet missed their target but his hands caught the end of the section and then he was hanging there— legs kicking, his arms flexing but unable to pull his body upward, and he was screaming for help—and the bridge was still coming together, coming down, dropping into place, and Rott's hands still clinging onto it, *right there for the amputation,* Gun thought.

"Let go! Take the water!" he shouted.

He watched the bridge lock together, heard its uncompromising sound, then ran to the edge in time to see Rott hit the surface of the Intracoastal and disappear. *Come up, come up,* then bob to the top again a few yards down, limbs flailing, wild screams coming from his throat. Gun looked toward shore. Already a boat was launched and heading in the right direction, police officers leaning forward in the bow.

Now Gun turned to the spot where he didn't want to look, the place where the bridge separated and joined, and saw there, still moving with life, a set of five fingers: pale, and indistinctly connected with whatever crush of bone and forearm must be locked in the bridge's jaws.

"Oh, my Lord." Gun looked away and then Diane Apple was in his arms, her hair against his face, the smell of it reminding him that the world was, after all, a place he didn't mind most of the time.

"We better call an ambulance or something." She pointed at Rott's fingers without looking, then ran to the edge of the bridge and threw up over the railing.

Below, Gun saw the policemen pulling Robert Weiler from the water into their boat.

38

Gun and Diane spent until four o'clock that afternoon at the police station going over Billy's notes again. Then, from a conversation with somebody at the D.A.'s office, he learned that Rott's trial wouldn't happen for a few months, and for now Gun was free to go home to Minnesota. At six-thirty he lay down on his bed in room number four of the Gates To Home Motel, thinking he needed a short nap; at eight the next morning he woke up, still fully clothed.

It was cowardly—Gun knew this—but he arranged to say good-bye to Diane at the airport, with Moses present. They met at nine for breakfast, the three of them, and spent the first half hour answering each other's questions. Mostly it was Moses doing the asking. He hadn't heard Billy's tapes.

"I don't believe it, I just don't believe it. Your brother, he was a bitchin' hard-ass, smart-headed writer, wasn't he? Had all that stuff underwater. I'm tellin' you, that *is* brilliant." Moses hadn't stopped smiling since he sat down, and once every few minutes he put on a deep scowl, probably just to keep his face from getting stuck. "I loved him," Moses said. "Billy was the sweetest guy I ever met, and I mean it, Diane." He reached across the table and took Diane's small wrists in his oversize hands. Then his smile crumpled and he shook his head and his whole body seemed to wither up. His shoulders fell, his chest sank away and the joy he'd been filled with fled the room.

"He thought a lot of you, too, Moses." Diane pressed her cheek against her own shoulder and looked away. Gun touched her on the back. "When we were kids," she said, "and you were Rookie of the Year, he always pretended he was you, every time he played ball. 'I'm Moses Gates,' he'd say and then cock his bat down low the way you did."

"I wasn't much more than a kid myself," said Moses. "And all this—it's not worth it. It isn't. None of it means a thing next to Billy."

"What it means," said Diane. "Billy wanted the truth and now we have it. Don't tell me that's not important. I couldn't bear to think it's not important. No, Moses, listen to me. I want everyone to know what he did and then I want to see you get voted into the Hall of Fame, just like you deserve and just like Billy wanted. And then maybe I'll be satisfied. Not that it's worth Billy's life, or that anything could be, but at least finally he will have accomplished what he set out to do. And that's important."

It was a rainy, overcast day, clouds low and ugly—a rare kind of day in this part of Florida—and Gun watched a plane leave the ground and disappear almost at once. He was anxious to be going. He felt no hope of resolution here. With Moses, yes, the man's life had gone from upside down to right side up, all in a few days. But not with Diane: grieving for her brother, looking to Gun for a kind of support he couldn't give. Not that he didn't want to. But the fact was, in some cases you couldn't help one person without letting someone else down miserably. It was a hard sticky little truth, but damn it all, there it was.

Gun took his hand away from Diane's shoulder now, looked at her small exquisite ear and asked her what she planned to do next. *What a dumb question.*

"Next? I don't know," she said, laughing just a little. "That word sounds funny, though. Kind of overconfident. Like there's always a next. A next day, a next job, a next life, a next whatever. I really don't know. How about you?"

Another plane disappeared and Gun looked at the clock. Ten-thirty. His flight wasn't departing for another forty-five minutes. "Life on the lake," Gun said, smiling, not feeling the words. He stood up then and said he had to leave, his plane was taking off in ten minutes.

Diane stood too and hugged him, asked him to please stay in touch. He said he would. Her arms didn't want to let go of him. His didn't want to let go of her, but he made them. Then he was shaking hands with Moses, not listening to the things Moses was saying about friendship and loyalty. And now he was walking quickly down the concourse, not turning to wave good-bye.

39

Asleep and drifting Gun floated back to the Gates To Home Motel, where he lay on his back trying to see the tiny gears of the blasted gas heater that had gone off again. Middle of the night and Florida was seeing weather like it hadn't since before the Spaniards slogged ashore in their chain mail. Had to be zero degrees, the windows stuck open and snow wisping in like the devil's tail and settling on the bed. Up in the dreamy recesses of the heater Gun thought he espied the sooty place where one lit the pilot light. With his fingers numb he scratched a match, got the thing going, then righted himself and kneeled by the register. The fan kicked in with a whirr and Gun put his face down to get the first warmth. What hit instead was an Alaskan wind that spat prickles of ice at his cheeks and he jerked back. The room was filling with snow and the gas heater had changed; now it was an air conditioner, decorator blue with a stylized carica-ture of Moses grinning on the front, and the logo: CHILL YOUR NOSE WITH A FROSTY-MOZE.

It took another snowy gust to sit him up and slap him back to where he was, in his own bed with the window cracked half an inch for sleeping and Minne-sota flexing its January muscles. He sat up. His bedroom faced east, and the wind was easterly, unusu-al; that was why it had come in so strongly. A little snow now but if the wind held there'd be some real weather. No unworkable gas burner in this house. He'd need a fire.

There was a good week's worth of wood split and dried in the breezeway between Gun's log house and garage. He went out in long johns and got an armload and kindling, got it snapping in the black stove and set coffee up to brew. The cold from the dream still had him by the joints, along with the stiffness adrenaline leaves behind like residue. He stretched some of it out and forced himself down to the bare wood floor for push-ups. They hurt his fists more than usual.

Diane Apple, blast her, he had been unnecessarily cool to her there at the end. Thought at the time it'd been best.

Well. It probably was. Still, Gun thought, his joints working looser now with the stove's close heat, it's so easy to see her here. Standing at the big paned windows at night with the light coming blue off the snow. He realized she had the grace that came with solitude, with knowing there's no crime in staying away from the mainstream. He finished his push-ups and sat back with the stiffness gone. He thought, You can't get a lot more solitary than this. She would approve, he thought, and it bothered him only a little that this mattered.

Carol Long arrived in midmorning carrying hot crusty bread and a mysterious plucked bird in a roasting pan. "Goose," she said, though it didn't look like it to Gun; too fat, not like the lanky birds he'd taken down in the fields of North Dakota.

"You're early."

"Haven't you heard? Snowstorm's on the way," she said, whirling off her knee-length leather coat. Today her lipstick was red as Christmas and her green eyes pranced so that he felt how long he'd been gone. She said, "Wouldn't it be something if I got snowed in?"

* * *

Catching her up on things took the rest of the morning and through the afternoon. They sat at the big maple table watching the frozen surface of Stony Lake go snow-cloud gray, she waiting out his silences for once instead of pushing in with questions. He told her how Rott Weiler, bigot, went over the top when he learned about Harold Ibbins's lineage; how he took that hate and fed it to Neil Faust, working it into a clubhouse loathing for Ferdie Millevich, the Minnesota boy with too much bat and too much conscience; how he made sure everyone would think he'd been out of town the day Ferdie died, and how the autograph man proved otherwise, all these years later.

"It's strange," he finished, "how it runs in the family. Rott's uncle, old Casper Leavitt—he's the one who paid off Faust to set up Ferdie and then Moses. Just another doting relative. His only regret is that he wasn't a little more subtle trying to get Billy Apple off the story. He sent those apes out to chase off the reporter—"

"And it just made Billy dig in harder," Carol said. "Yes."

The clouds were putting an early end on the afternoon. Out on Stony they could just see the distant fish houses and pickup trucks, the little black figures moving slowly about. Gun could smell the fat goose roasting and the warmth of it along with Carol's nearness gave him a sense of discomfort, of fleeting claustrophobia, like wearing too many sweaters.

"It almost seems," she said, her words sounding vaguely awkward to Gun, "like you really knew Billy Apple. Like you met him. Doesn't it?"

"Mmm." It did and it didn't. When it came down to it, Gun realized, it was Billy's sister he was glad he'd met.

"I'm freezing," she said suddenly. He took her hand

and it was true. He cupped her fingers in his and blew on them, a gentle father-daughter gesture. It had always warmed her before, made her smile. Now it didn't.

"You're distracted," she told him. He was. He was busy realizing, with guilt growing in him like an ache, that he wished Diane would somehow appear. That she'd just show up, drive in smiling through the big pines. Or write him a letter, even. Or call him.

Call him.

"Hard time down south," he said.

"That's it?" Carol asked.

"That's it."

"Well," she said, letting down some. "Over now."

When the buzzer went off a little later she said, "The goose." But it was the phone ringing in the middle of her sentence that really got his attention.

40

Not Diane, though.

Rott Weiler, calling collect, from his plain square room in the hospital. Gun knew the voice even though it seemed notched up somehow, skidding ahead word to word.

"Gun, you gotta listen to me. I got some serious trouble here."

"I'll go along with that."

"I'm not talkin' about jail, Pedersen. I can take jail. But nobody's listenin' to me—not my lawyer, even.

I'm telling you, I killed Ferdie Millevich—but I never touched Billy Apple, or the Ibbinses."

"Rott. I'm hanging up."

The voice clicked up another notch. "I'm not dodging blame. If I hadn't done Ferdie, God help me, the others wouldn't have been necessary. But I didn't do the killings, not these last ones."

Carol was watching Gun and he saw her understand, even as he did, that this wasn't all over. Not yet.

He said, "Who's with you there?"

"Nobody. They brought in a private line. My lawyer did that much." A little of the old peevish Rott.

"All right, go ahead. Who's got the dirty hands?"

"You know him. My uncle, Casper Leavitt."

Gun was quiet. It was the only answer Rott could've given that didn't deserve a hang-up. He needed time to think.

"Explain Ferdie, first."

"I thought it was the only way." Rott leapt into it without pause or any attempt at self-justification. As if, Gun thought, he had to get through it fast before he could make whatever pitch Gun knew was coming. "Ferdie'd figured it out, what Neil Faust and I did to him. He was gonna take it public." His tone changed. "It ain't like some people say, Pedersen. You murder once, you don't wanna do it again."

"So you had Casper fix the others."

"Yes, goddamnit. Yes. Apple wouldn't quit. He had Faust by the nose hairs. I didn't go to Casper, though —he came to me, wondered if he could help. I thought he was gonna freeze Apple off the story somehow, you know? I didn't know he was gonna use Louis. Louis, he's always a mistake. He likes to tie his knots."

Gun remembered the man, the animal lights in the corners of his eyes. "Louis killed Harold, too? Miss Mary?"

"That's right."

"So I guess the question, Rott, is what am I supposed to do about all this? Why call me?"

The skidding fear came off Rott's voice altogether and he said it slowly: *"My uncle is going to kill me."*

Gun found this an easy thing to believe. Casper had plenty to hide. "Tell the police."

"Listen. Today I'm in the big room here, eating my dinner, and the orderly next to me, I've never seen him before. I'm leanin' over sayin', 'Pass the salt;' and this guy leans into me just enough so I've got something sharp under my bottom rib, and he says to me, 'Casper's got no ratfinks among his kin.' That's all. He don't need to say more."

"Like I said, Rott: Why call me?"

"Like *I* said: You know my uncle. You think I didn't hear about your little war out there? There ain't nobody here got the ears for it when I say he'll have me cut before I get to trial. But you dealt with him. You talked to him. You know it's so."

The goose for all its fat was not as tender as the wild kind and worse there was none of the good arch flavor of field and long migration. Gun had learned to mellow a wild bird with a ripe orange split in the deep cavity and strips of bacon laid over the breast to roast; Carol had done the same with this goose, but the domesticated meat was floored by the attention and barely showed up at all except as a sponge for bacon and cooked orange. Still Gun ate willingly and for Carol's sake attempted heartiness, without success. The last of daylight folded into low clouds and flurries. She cleared the table away in silence, poured them coffee. Finally she said, "I don't think you're ready to be home."

"Don't know what to do. It scrapes me to believe Rott, but I think he's being honest."

"So what will you do? Fly back south?"

It had crossed his mind. Not in connection with Rott, though.

"Think it over, I guess. He wants me to bargain with his uncle, tell him Rott won't squeal on him as long as Casper pays his legal defense fees on all four murder charges."

Carol frowned. "If all this is true, why doesn't Rott bargain with Casper himself?"

"He says he's tried, that Casper won't talk. And now this guy tickles his ribs, gives him a warning. On the other hand, if I go talk to Casper, then Casper's got to wonder who else knows about it. Maybe that's Rott's thinking."

They sat in the yellow-pine light of the kitchen, thinking thoughts as separate and whirling as the flakes coming fast now outside.

"Gun, couldn't somebody nail Casper another way? What about those relatives of Clarence Coldspring's that he buried in the swamp?"

"They were so long ago. Somebody'd have to pursue it, and even the Coldsprings aren't interested in that. They found the bodies, remember, and they just buried them again."

Carol smiled, rose, went for her coat. "Well. You let me know what you decide. You fly south, maybe I could find someone to baby-sit the newspaper if you want company. Otherwise, I'll be home."

He turned on the outside floodlight and saw how white the air was getting. "What happened to getting snowed in?"

"Do you want me to be?" Her coat on already.

He let himself hesitate and she reached him a kiss, said, "Do what you have to for Rott and not an ounce more," and left with snow sweeping past him through the door.

Later, Gun would admit to himself that Rott's predicament that night didn't cost him too much

peace, except for one tiny back-of-the-mind moment
when he knew, just before sleep reached up and pulled
him in, that there were times you told the truth too
late, and then it didn't matter.

41

Sometime during the night Gun's mind gave over its
reluctance and he woke early planning to go back,
what the hell, and give Casper a go. Maybe it would
keep Rott off somebody's spit, although Gun didn't
delude himself that his decision was based on mercy.
Maybe, he thought, going south would raise other
opportunities; a chance to pay off Casper for killing
Billy Apple. A way to make the old man see that
sending a madman to toss Harold Ibbins off his roof
and shoot his wife through a mattress had been the
wrong, wrong thing to do.

The snow, though. It was going like a carnival now,
filling up the panes on his lakeside windows. He'd
have to wait it out. Diane came to his mind again and
he allowed himself to miss her. It sweetened his coffee,
and when the phone rang he knew it was her, let it ring
an extra time so he wouldn't seem hurried.

"Gun. It's Diane."

Yes, but the voice was wrong. Shaking all over the
place, and some idiot restaurant music in the background.

"Gun, it's really bad . . . what's happened, it's impossible, but listen: They came out to the boat—"

"Who? Who came to the boat?"

"Casper's guys. Last night, maybe two o'clock. It was a beautiful moon, I was out walking the dock . . . and I heard them drive up. Three men. They came straight for the boat and I jumped into the cockpit of an empty cruiser or they'd have seen me. Gun, they went into the *Napper* looking for me. I could hear them laughing as they stepped aboard. Saying horrible things. Then when I was gone I heard shouting, and they came up grim and took off. I didn't dare go back on board." Diane's voice had calmed some but now went watery with fright. "I was still standing there when the whole back end of the *Napper* blew off. Like when you're a kid, you blow tin cans apart with firecrackers, that's what it was like. The whole transom lit up and stood out by itself on the water, and then in ten seconds the boat was down."

Gun felt a dry swallow crawl down his throat. "Where are you now? I'll come."

"Don't. I'm on the road, and as long as I stay this way I'm out of trouble. Listen and I'll tell you how lucky I am. I was driving up the coast half an hour ago with the radio on and got the news. Rott Weiler's dead. Right there in his room. You want to guess how?"

Gun shut his eyes. "Hanged. Right." Thinking: The wheel turns.

"This is the worst part. It's Clarence. The police found him in a ditch last night, partly covered over. He'd been tortured, burns all over his body."

It made Gun sting with the memory of the prod and Christian's moans. He felt it again, too, all along his arms. "Dead?"

"Not yet. Apparently they thought he was. He's in intensive."

"I'm coming."

"Wait. This is the thing: Rott knew all about Casper, and now Rott's dead. Clarence only knew part of it, and they got to him. They're trying for me. Gun, you're last on the list. They're not going to forget you."

The phone at Jack Be Nimble's rang tiredly on until Jack picked it up and said "LaSalle" in his I-don't-open-till-eleven voice.

"It's Gun."

"Hey. You got back just in time, we got a blizzard here."

"Yup. Makes you wish you were back in school, listening for the closings. Jack, that old Scout of yours still run?"

"Such questions you ask."

Gun reached into a drawer for tobacco and papers. He rolled as he spoke. "Down Florida way I met a gentleman who is unused to disruptions in his routine."

"Naturally, you bumbled into his path," Jack said. "Don't tell me you left something undone down there."

"It's something I'd rather tell you about in person. I have reason to suppose that this gentleman has asked some friends of his to visit me."

Jack went serious. "You really got people after you? This have anything to do with that Faust fellow who went through the crust?"

"Long story, and it never seems to end." Gun inhaled and felt the calm tobacco work. Outside his window a long pine limb gave under a foot of new snow, let go with a muffled crack and landed in a waist-high drift. "I don't think anyone's going to come calling while the storm's on. Maybe they won't come at all. But I want to be ready."

There was quiet on the line and then Jack said, "Take me a while in this weather. The Scout never dies, though. Gun—you think I should bring some fireworks?"

"Jack. Such questions you ask."

42

By ten-thirty Gun had swallowed enough coffee to slow down every clock in the house and still Jack hadn't arrived. Wasn't answering his phone, either. Three hours was more than enough time to make seven miles. Weather or not. Gun layered on wool pants and shirts, pulled on an army parka still stained from the last World War and over it all the pure white wind-shell his daughter, Mazy, said made him look like the Abominable Snowman. He'd bought the wind-shell for hunting snow geese, for lying in the fields among the white-rag decoys until the birds were in range and he rose up for them, but he wore it most in winter. It sealed the army parka's gappy seams.

The wind stripped the storm door from his grasp when he opened it, slamming it wide and wrenching the closing mechanism off the doorjamb. Ungodly cold. He grabbed for it, tried to get it shut but another blast tore it away again and this time the hinges went and the door hung an instant before separating from the house and skimming over the snow like a kite. It hit a rock at the edge of Stony Lake and the glass shattered. Gun made sure the inside door was latched and worked his way along the house. The wind drove tiny hard-edged flakes into his eyes, his nostrils. Snow filled his tracks almost as fast as he made them. He reached the garage. The old Ford pickup sat within, backed against the workbench on the rear wall like it knew what was out there and wanted no part of it. He heaved open the big front door and saw four-foot drifts and waves for at least fifty feet before the pines started blocking the wind.

He'd never bothered to get a snowblower. "I like the work," he'd told Mazy.

He didn't like it this much. He closed the door, told himself he'd take a little walk down the driveway, see if he saw headlights out on the tar. Then go in and try calling Jack again. Then, start shoveling.

Halfway down the drive he saw headlights turn in off the blacktop and thought, *He made it,* but that was before he saw a second set of headlights, and a third. They came toward him slowly, towering four-wheel-drives rumbling in redneck satisfaction. He stepped off the driveway behind a slender pine. How had they made it so fast? Rott not dead twenty-four hours, Diane's near-miss only this morning. The trucks stopped, killed lights and engines and Gun thought at first they'd seen him. *No. They'll walk in. Of course.*

Squatting in the snow he counted six of them. Heavily parka'd and armed. They convened briefly at the cab of the lead truck, then split into pairs and came, rifles cradled in their arms, the barrels glistening through the snow. Gun stood and tried to step back farther into the trees. He couldn't. The little pine had snagged the hood of the wind-shell. The men came on. He yanked but the snag was up where he couldn't see it. Twenty yards away he heard their voices high in the rough wind. Then a gust threw a curtain of white across the drive, and Gun let his weight fall back and the snag let go, dropping him soundlessly into a drift. He rolled onto his stomach, breathed in ice, pulled the white hood forward. Waited.

They said nothing as they went by, six feet to his left.

His breath, except when he held it to let them tramp past, melted a tiny iced depression in the snow.

When he looked up, snowy browed, he saw by the slope-shaped parka rising over the others that Louis had come along north.

He saw them reach the house and walk into it without so much as peeking through a window. The weather gave them confidence. He made the best time he could getting back to their trucks. Unlocked, all of them, but the cautious bastards had taken their keys. Every weapon, too—a check under seats yielded one brass cartridge, .30-.30 caliber. Spent. On impulse Gun looked in the beds of the trucks. They were half full of sand, covered with a layer of new snow. In bad winters Gun had sometimes done the same thing with the old Ford. Traction.

He went with the wind into the pines and leaned against one, his forehead against the ruddy bark. *Inspect the circumstances.* He was weaponless, without a vehicle. He couldn't leave on foot—he'd seen too many blizzards, knew he couldn't fight this one when he reached the open ground. Besides, Jack was coming. Probably be here soon. And his attackers—who he'd been expecting, who he'd prepared for by laying out his old Model 12 and two boxes of double-ought upon the kitchen table—these men were *inside* the house, laughing at his little arsenal, drinking coffee from his stove. Waiting for him.

Where in the name of Heaven was Jack?

A shred of wind snake tailed down Gun's back and he realized the wind-shell was coming undone from where it had snagged earlier. The cold told him he couldn't wait long. *Move.* He could go back to the garage, look for a weapon. Fight six men with a tire iron? No. Besides, it was too near the house; put a guy near the right window, they'd see him. The boat house, maybe. Yes, the stone boat house. He closed his eyes, trying to see what he'd left in the place when he closed it up in the fall.

He saw enough to move.

It was a twenty-minute circuit through the woods and down to the shore. He navigated tree-to-tree, the house sometimes coming into view when the wind lulled. Then he could see lights burning in the windows, an occasional shape going by. They looked warm.

He got to the boat house at last, the stone-and-wood shelter finally showing itself when he got within fifteen yards of it. The padlock was frozen, the keyhole stuffed with snow. He took his time, put his mouth to the lock, blew. The metal stuck to his lips. He kept blowing. Five breaths later the lock came off his mouth and he got the key in, turned slowly and felt the give.

Inside, calm. Looking about him in the low light from the single snow-plugged window Gun praised the silence. *The wind's a voice at your ear, all the time there until you can't think with it and you commit your last mistake.* Slamming the boat house door he'd shut the voice up, forced it to the background. Now he scavenged among summer stuff, marine tools, oars, the dented Alumacraft. From his tackle box he took a spool of woven forty-pound test line and a fillet knife. He used the knife to free his anchor, a folding Danforth all points and edges, from its nylon rope. He rummaged in the dark rafters with his bare fingers until he found long cold steel and brought it down: an old triple-tined fishing spear, its middle tooth gone but two still thick and strong like barbed fangs. He'd broken it the winter before, missing a pike and hitting a big quartz rock on the bottom. Had meant to fix it but instead went out and uncharacteristically bought a new one, a big four-pointer.

Four points or two. If the fish was big enough, it didn't matter.

He was ready ten minutes later and felt for the first time a charge of real fear, as if the cold were radiating out from his belly. His fingers shook in the big leather mitts. Carrying the spear and a lidless Folgers coffee can he went out the lakeside door. The wind spoke again but he did not listen. He reached up with the spear and swept clear a space on the roof, the new shingles showing black and green. He'd built the boat house himself, only last summer. He leaned the spear against the side and used the Folgers can to slosh gasoline on the shingles. Hateful work. Most of it ran off and he got more from the red tank in the Alumacraft. When he had it done he went in the boat house one last time, dropped a lit match into the can, carried it out with his mitts on, and tossed it to the roof.

43

The *whoom* of the gas going up was all but drowned by the wind, but the tar shingles had absorbed enough to catch and hold the fire that ripped and danced against the storm. Flames leapt up ten feet, twenty, threatened to hush, then built up slow and hot as Gun hastily wrapped his oars in gas-drenched rags and laid them over the roof. In minutes the fire didn't smell of fuel anymore but of tar and scorching kiln-dried pine, and even in the storm Gun felt the heat of it. He crouched at the corner of the lake-stone hut, watching the house, trusses roaring above him. It took longer than it should have. About the time he was starting to think, *Too late, much longer and the roof's gonna go,* his front door swung open and he ducked out of sight.

Two men. The hoods of their parkas were drawn up like blinders and they held rifles crossways on their chests as they waded down through the snow. *Pick it up, move, go fast, go hard. Go in.* Gun flattened against the stones. Held the forked spear close so the frozen tines pressed his cheek. Sensed the men as they reached the opposite side of the boat house from where he stood. *In.* He felt the tremor of the door being yanked open and needing to trust his plan lowered the spear and stepped around the corner. There was a thump and a windblown yell and he saw one of them stooping over the other where he lay half-in, half-out, the open door. He charged the one standing, the deep snow slowing him to madness until at last the guy looked up gaping, one armed his rifle to point at exactly the place where the wind-shell's zipper opened to the throat and tried to fire but was delayed by mittened fingers just long enough to take the spear in the soft V beneath the rib cage. The man released his gun and a warble of high-pitched panic that made Gun loathe himself, but he grabbed for the rifle anyway, seeing as he did so the first man lying in the doorway senseless, the Danforth anchor on its side by his head. It had gone the way it had to. He realized now that the side of his face toward the boat house was cooking and he looked up to see the entire roof ablaze and screaming with the abundance of oxygen. With the spitted man gone quiet and a sense of debt he knew was misplaced Gun let go of the rifle and pulled the unconscious man out before the fire fell in on him. Then a chunk of rock next to his head blew itself into fine gray rain and he heard the far-off crackle of gunfire like popcorn in the storm. Men on his porch, shooting, swinging their coats on, and he dove on his face behind the corner of the boat house. And saw another gun. Pointed at him. In a hand that held him solid in the sights until he peered up and beheld its short square-bodied owner.

"Jack," Gun said.

The pistol lowered. "Better late," said Jack LaSalle.

"Maybe," said Gun, and then they were away down the jagged shore of Stony Lake, keeping the boat house between themselves and the rifles, knowing only the clean brute cut of the air in their throats and the drag of the snow as they ran.

A quarter mile, a half. They'd left the open shore for the cover of trees, but it cost them speed and there was no covering or confusion of trail in such snow. Two feet of stiff powder. It was like trying to run with rubber hobbles on your ankles.

"Warrior Point," Gun gasped. His lungs filled, froze, plunged, said *don't mess with us no more.*

Jack nodded with his head and shoulders and kept the pace. Warrior Point Resort, a few hundred yards farther on. Old place, abandoned a few years back. Not the Alamo exactly but lots of empty buildings, and Jack had a pistol.

And then he didn't anymore. They crossed a small clear space in the pines where the wind stopped completely, and going through it was like moving across another season in a world that bore no noise, and just as they reached the trees again there was a small white hiss of bullet. Gun saw Jack look down at his hand, saw him register disbelief and stumble briefly until anger lifted him straight again and made him keep on. Blood sickled rhythmically onto the snow before him and Gun saw that he plowed the last ten yards into Warrior Point with his eyes jammed closed before holding up his right hand. It was bare, stripped of gun and leather glove, and where Jack's thick index finger had been was a deep crimson hollow, like an empty eye socket filling with blood.

44

The first cabin they tried was locked, the door too heavy and well-bolted for any he-man nonsense, but the cabin nearest the lake had been roundly vandalized and opened up like a dead clam. Jack said, "Can't stop here," but his face was white and it was plain they had to. Gun had the wind-shell off, ripped a strip out of the back, ran to the door, scooped a handful of snow.

"Pressure," he said. He took Jack's plundered hand and packed the wound with snow, then wound it as tightly as he could with the cloth and told Jack to hold it while he used what chairs there were to block the door closed.

"Yah," Jack said. He sat on the cigarette-scarred Formica of the kitchen table, rocking the pain. Behind him on the wall was an attempt at obscenity and a slogan in fuzzy copper spray paint: UNDERACHIEVERS, CLASS OF '91. Gun was suddenly busy at the stove, a ceramic-white antique connected to a tall steel cylinder. "Gun," Jack said, "they're gonna get here in about three seconds. You gonna have them in for coffee?"

Gun had all four burners hissing. "There's still gas.

Smell." He turned back to the stove, sniffed. "Not fast enough." Not bothering to turn off the burners he bent, test rocked the stove once, got a grip, and lifted. It twisted free of the wall and the cylinder tipped and fell, crinkling the copper pipe that fed gas to the stove. The hiss got louder.

"What, more fires?" Jack said.

"Maybe it gets their minds off us. Maybe it gets somebody else's attention."

"Maybe we're out of smarts." Jack coughed into his hands.

The gas was enough now to scorch the lungs, shrivel the lining of the nostrils. Almost there. Breathing shallow as a kitten Gun grappled the big cylinder to a standing position. Lifted it cleanly, balanced it on his palms. Heard two firm knocks at the front door, almost polite, and the voice of Casper Leavitt: "Hello, Pedersen. Don't this weather make the snot run?" Then he jerked the cylinder up over his head and brought it down hard on the edge of the stove, straight across the nozzle. Ceramic finish splintered, something hit the door with the weight of a black bear forcing it half a foot open, and the gas hiss became a full loose-nozzled squeal. "A match," Gun whispered. He'd used his last sending up the boat house.

"Don't have one," Jack said. The back door was just off the kitchen and without time to wonder who was watching it Gun and Jack slammed through and went for the trees. Behind them they heard the front door crash and go to ruin and the little cabin crowd up. The real air was a relief but underfoot the snow seemed stickier, heavier, murderous to run through. Gun's breath was shortening and he willed the reserves to open but they were all through, caverns filled with sand. He slowed. Jack clutched at his right hand and his eyes were closed again. But there was no chase, not yet, and in the sparse-standing trees still too near the cabin Gun turned and saw why.

Louis had him in his sights. He was standing in the kitchen, just far enough back from the window to raise his large-bore rifle. Gun saw the foreshortened weapon lying easy in Louis's big hands. There were lines of pleasure at the corners of his eyes, a little shine of tooth showing next to the trigger guard. Gun recognized the restless shift of shoulder as Louis started to squeeze. In that trigger-hair of time Gun wondered how he could breathe in all that gas, and then he dove and Louis fired. At the barrel's tip he saw the tiny spark of flame, then the barrel disappeared in the sun white clot of fire that was suddenly the kitchen window. The clot was a pure square of glory until its own *whoosh* reached his ears, then it burst with a monstrous crunching explosion that brought the roof a foot off the walls, light coming out the crack between before it fell back, off center, leaning, and there was no more noise.

A few shy flames explored along the roof-ridge of the cabin. At the kitchen window, no sign of Louis. Gun sat in the snow, seeing it gray now instead of white. After the fireball, nothing could look so bright. He looked over at Jack, who'd been blown off his feet. He'd forgotten about his hand and the bandage was coming unwrapped, bleeding again. Gun thought he had never understood the gift that was destruction.

And they got to their feet and went to the cabin, which after the shock was just settling into a good burn, and there found that Casper had somehow lived. He sat upright upon his butt in the snow, five feet outside the doorway he'd been lucky enough to be blown through. His thick brows were bunched over eyes gone bloody and sightless and he held his heavy arms straight out from the shoulders, tentatively, the arms tipping and balancing like a ropewalker's. His face was beflecked with bits of Louis.

"Casper," Gun said.

"Oof," Casper said in the loud voice of the newly deaf. "Louis."

Gun said, "Can you see anything? Hear?"

Casper slowly pulled in his wings and folded them like a child in a storm. His legs were disappearing in the still-heavy snow.

This time Gun shouted. "Casper!"

It got through. "Pedersen?"

"Yes!"

Hearing now, however faintly, Casper lowered his voice. He shook his head, made no attempt to stand. "I guess you'll be braggin' now," he said. "Do you know, I never lost before, and now here it is. Oof. I can't even see. My ass is freezing off and I can't even watch it go. *Louis!*"

"Dead!" Gun said, bending to Casper's ear.

"Yes. He would be." Casper ungloved a hand and reached up, stroked blood off his well-bred nose. "Never owned a mind, that one. What I'm tellin' you, you try to pass on the attributes you got, improve the family, but sometimes it don't take. Now the other fellows—dead, all of them?"

Gun looked at Jack dragging a half-conscious man out the cabin door. There was groaning. Not loud enough for Casper to hear.

"Not all," Gun said.

"You'll be wanting to finish it, then," said Casper. It didn't seem to bother him. He sat waiting, not blinking as snowflakes landed in his eyes.

Gun crouched again, the cold getting to him now like he was back in the freeze of Jack Knife Lake. He shouted into Casper's ear, *"You're an old man. You should die at home."*

"Oof, shit," said Casper.

45

Actually three of them lived, though none felt good enough to be all that happy about it. Casper had gone to muttering and casting his arms about in the dark around him; the other two needed salve and tape and a little hot chicken broth in Gun's kitchen. Funny, how the malice disappeared now that the old man was too weak to stir it up.

The snow kept dropping down, piling up high on the eaves and branches, not drifting so much since the wind had died. Jack sat on a kitchen stool with his disinfected right hand knotted in his left. Casper's men drank broth in silence, likely thinking of the others. There'd been two of them whole, and then what they could find of Louis, and all of this they buried in the sand in the bed of one of the pickup trucks. When the broth was gone they saw that Casper had dropped to sleep in his straight-backed chair, and the bigger man picked him up like a midnight child and carried him out to his truck. Two drivers meant they had to leave one of the overbuilt trucks behind. They didn't speak of it. Just started up, backed out onto the highway, and rumbled off slowly in respect of the snow.

Gun thought of going to the phone, of course, and dialing the State Police. *You boys might want to watch for a couple of big four-wheelers, sporting Florida plates and heading south. If you care to have a look, you'll find they're loaded with sand and dead men.* But then he thought about the questions they'd have for him. Hours of questions. Days. Like who *are* these guys anyway, and why are some of them dead? And why didn't you call us earlier? And though Gun had the answers, the right ones, he didn't have the will or the strength at this point to put them into words. Instead, he sat at the table letting his coffee go cold and he pictured Casper slouched on the bench seat of the truck, fighting himself through a troubled, coughing sleep. He pictured the abandoned vehicle in the snow outside the cabin and schemed half a dozen ways to make it disappear. Within an hour's drive were tracts of forest, vast and dense and penetrated only by overgrown logging trails. Just drive in a mile or two and park it. There was also the lake, deep, more than a hundred and fifty feet in places. Plenty of other vehicles down there already, too.

He stayed away from the phone.

The strangest thing about not having any food in the house was how long Gun took to notice it. Two days went by in which he slept late, then rose and went into the poststorm newness to walk dreaming in the snow. To believe the landscape, none of it had happened; only the fires. His boat house was a mess, a stone foundation filled with hull and cinders, and the cabin at Warrior Point was plain gone except for the melted appliances. Nobody'd even noticed it yet. You want help, never have a fire in a blizzard.

On the third day Gun noticed that his push-ups lacked definition. They bobbed a little, and there weren't as many of them. He sat up, felt the whiskers on his cheeks. He thought, *Oh. Food.*

But there wasn't anything, just some buttermilk that had been in the fridge since before the call from Moses and a little of Carol's cold goose. He tossed it out.

Two hours' shoveling freed the old Ford and had

him shaking with a weakness he somehow recognized. It seemed to him more than exhaustion and hunger, more than the aftershock of fear and proximity of death. It was, he thought suddenly, the soul of cold itself, and it had turned on him. Before, the purity of cold had always worked for him, given his lungs the clean shock they seemed to need; cold simmered his blood and lifted his brain. In the cold he'd worked his hardest, and loved it. And now, somehow, it was different. The frozen air tapped his strength and muddied thought. Cold was a thing to be survived.

The truck's old engine started without a fight, knocked around a little and evened down into a comfortable roar. Gun steered it out of the garage, turned the heater on with the fan low until things warmed up. Shivering hollow-gutted inside the parka he fought the cold. *It's this snow,* he thought, *that's the difference. There's too much blood in it.*

He bought bright red meat in Stony, a chilly bagful of it, and also some pale broccoli and asparagus, potatoes, milk, Swiss Miss. He passed a pyramid of oranges that were somehow fresh and the scent gave him Diane for a moment and his gut warmed, but only briefly. The checkout girl looked at him for too long on the way out, as if his face gave her worries she didn't need.

The way home took him past the newspaper and Carol's office. He drove slowly and saw her faithful Plymouth, angle parked. She'd be there, she said it herself, if he wanted company.

Too soon to be sure about that.

At home he started a modest roast: seared it on both sides, the noise of it rising like steam in his ears, the beef smell almost pain. When red had gone to deep brown he added pepper, salt, water from the kettle. Potatoes, some of the asparagus. He left the kitchen for the davenport and lay down. There was sun on the windows. With the storm gone away February had entered Minnesota, and Gun knew he'd feel March coming on sooner than usual this year.

Sweet Lord, how he needed to.

In the kitchen the roast began to fret and bubble. Gun hunched himself into the davenport, closed his eyes. *When the dark hours come, sleep, sleep long.*

About the Author

L. L. Enger lives in Minnesota. He bats, throws and shoots right-handed. His first book, *Comeback,* was nominated for an Edgar Award. He is working on another Gun Pedersen novel for Pocket Books.

JEREMIAH HEALY

A John Cuddy Mystery
RIGHT TO DIE

"...one of the most appealing writers in the business."—*Boston Globe*

It's Christmastime in Boston, the fifty-foot tree is up on Boylston Street, and an old friend has just contacted Cuddy to ask a favor. Tommy Kramer and Cuddy go way back—to combat in Vietnam, the death of Cuddy's young wife, and an innocent but serious brush with the law. There' no refusing such a friend's request. Maisy Andrus, the woman Kramer wants Cuddy to help, has made one too many enemies crusading for the individual's inalienable right to die. So as winter takes the city in its icy wraps, Cuddy is trying to protect a headstrong, flamboyant woman from a potential assassin, and trying to stay alive long enough to take on the Boston Marathon.

**Available in Hardcover
From Pocket Books**